ROMANCING A WALLFLOWER

NOBLE HEARTS BOOK 2

ANNA ST. CLAIRE

ANNA ST. CLAIRE

Cover Design by Dar Albert, Wicked Smart Designs

Editor and Historical Consultant – Heather King

DEDICATION & REMEMBRANCES

Dedicated to my own special hero, Roger, who without fail, makes sure that each and every day we spend together is nothing short of our own happily ever after. Thank you for giving me the space and the encouragement to pursue my passion.

A special tribute to our sweet Cooper—my daughter's dog. He is a gentle and beloved dog that will always own a piece of my heart. Certainly, he has his own special place in this story and the cover.

And a special remembrance to Rascal, my mother's beloved dog—a beloved pet from my childhood that taught us the love and devotion of animals, and who will always be a part of my mother's heart, as well as my sister's and mine.

ROMANCING A WALLFLOWER

NOBLE HEARTS - BOOK 2

Once in a while, in the middle of an ordinary life, love gives us a fairytale.

—Unknown

PROLOGUE

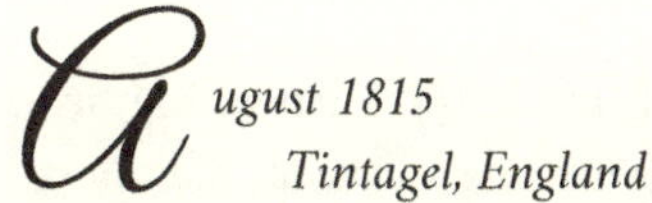

ugust 1815
Tintagel, England

"That was a narrow escape! I thought Chambers was going to tell us Mama was looking for us." Lydia DeLacey put her hand to her mouth, smothering her giggles as she joined her twin sister at the bottom of the front steps of their father's house.

"Hurry!" Lilian urged. Picking up their skirts, they ran down the gravel path to the stables, arriving breathless and intoxicated with excitement at avoiding Mama's machinations. Two handsome gentlemen had arrived earlier to meet with their father. The twin's abigail, who had had it from Cook, had told her mistress that Mama had ordered tea to be served at four of the clock.

Lilian hated to think her father would arrange marriages for her sister and herself—not when he and their mother still enjoyed a love match. However, her mother was notorious for *creating opportunities*, as she termed it, for her two daughters to meet the men of their dreams and seemed determined, despite Lilian and her twin showing no interest in any of their suitors, to find at least one match.

Her joyous mood changed when she saw the head groom waiting at the door of the stables.

"Oh, marvellous! Barney is waiting for us," she muttered with a hint of sarcasm.

"We will have to take him, Lilian."

She yearned to ride Danby, the dark bay she had brought on from birth. She loved the fresh air and thrilled to the independence riding her horse gave her. Often, she and Lydia rode neck and neck, racing over the pastures and fields of her parent's estate. Such freedom was impossible in London.

"Good morning, my lady and my lady." Barney, the head groom, stepped forward with their horses. "I took the liberty of having Danby and Ginger saddled. I thought you would wish to ride this morning. Me own horse is also ready." He sent an imploring look in their direction.

Lilian glanced at her sister and then around her, struggling to find an excuse to leave him behind. There was none, although on many an occasion she and her sister had contrived to lose him. The poor man knew they were likely to put him through his paces.

"Thank you, Barney." Lilian smiled tightly. "It is a beautiful day for a ride, is it not? We will endeavour not to trouble you unduly."

"Yes, my lady." He noticeably gulped and led Lydia's horse to the mounting block. He helped each of them onto their horse and climbed upon his own. The small party rode out of the stable yard, Lilian and her sister in the lead and the groom trailing a safe distance behind.

Flowers were in bloom everywhere. A purple blanket of creeping thyme edged the path. Bluebells and bright yellow cat's ear carpeted the sides of the hill, dominating small sunny areas as it climbed a ridge beyond them, making the small pockets of pink wild roses very noticeable.

"This is truly lovely, Lil. The air even feels cooler. It is perfect weather for our ride," Lydia commented.

"Would you care to ride to the cliffs today?" Lilian questioned.

"I would love to, but do you think we should? Father has asked us to stay close to the house. He does not want us near the cliffs unchaperoned because of the free traders. I do not think he would consider Barney sufficient protection."

Lilian did not care to bear Father's wrath. He was normally a gentle soul, but when it was needful, he could become intractable.

She agreed with her sister. "Yes, the thought of Barney defending our honour is almost too much to contemplate. Very well. What about the ruins? We could follow the ridge and mayhap stretch the horses there."

"That is a good plan. Mama will be so cross! I wonder who these gentlemen are?"

"An earl and his friend, Father said this morning. You were too busy eyeing that new footman to notice."

"Perhaps we should have taken the Season more seriously and she would not be so frantic about our finding suitable matches," Lydia replied. The family had arrived home from London only a week ago and had barely unpacked.

Lilian sighed. "There *was* one gentleman…"

"Oh, I know the one you mean, and I noticed *your* reaction to him. He was wearing his regimental dress although, according to Mama, he is an earl."

Lilian was not surprised Lydia knew exactly the man she remembered. It had been the last ball of the Season. She drew in a breath, recalling how she had noticed him the moment he had entered the room.

"I will admit I wished he would ask me to dance, but he and his friend did not seem to remain long."

"Quite. I noticed him watching you and thought he would ask to be introduced, but then his friend came back with glasses of champagne, said something to him and they left."

"Perhaps there was an emergency." Her mind flitted back to that night. "They were both interesting, but so were several others. I noticed you seemed taken with Viscount Yarstone." Although she spoke the words, Lilian's mind was still on the gentleman in the regimentals.

"Do come down from the clouds, sister," Lydia teased.

Wrinkling her nose at Lydia, Lilian gave her horse a slight nudge, sending him into a canter. Her hat came off and she felt her hair fall from its pins until her long auburn brown curls were flowing behind her. She did not care. She had Danby, and she was here on this glorious morning. It was all that mattered.

Her sister looked behind them. "Good heavens! Barney is keeping up!" Immodestly, Lydia yelled across the space between them, gesturing with a jerk of her head and obviously goading Lilian to look.

Instead, Lilian sniggered in a rude way and gave Danby another nudge. Her brown gelding ran faster, forcing Lydia and her chestnut to race to catch them. It felt wondrous. The two sisters rode across the crest of the hill for a good while, deftly dodging trees, fences and outcrops of rock—doggedly followed, some distance behind, by their groom. Low shrubs and weathered post-and-rail fencing bordered one edge of the path they followed, and masses of coloured flowers covered the ground, gradually disappearing from sight.

A more wooded area appeared in a bend in the track ahead of them, and as they approached, a loud shot rang out. Danby shied violently sideways and with a shrill squeal of distress, reared high on his back legs.

"Lilian!" Lydia cried out.

Lilian heard her sister's cry and was dimly aware of her struggles to gain control over Ginger, but her own struggle to maintain her seat was failing. Somehow, her legs loosened from the pommels of her side-saddle when the horse rose, and she fought to keep her balance. Danby lost his footing and as he toppled, the force of him hitting the earth tossed her to the ground. She landed on a stone, or something equally hard, the momentum then rolling her across the rough ground until she thudded into a large rock. She heard her own scream pierce the air.

Lydia and the groom tried to lift her, but she screamed in pain at their touch. Although she could see them speaking to her, their voices sounded distant. Her vision was growing darker and she could barely see; she was viewing their faces and the sky behind them through a small, dark hole which kept shrinking. Her world was growing dark. Her head and her back ached fiercely. Her ears were ringing. She wanted to scream and tried yet could hear nothing. Pain throbbed from every part of her body. She tried to move, to get up, but her feet...*what was wrong with her feet?* They were not moving. What had she done? Her head pounded, and warm liquid ran down the side of her face. A large warm hand grasped hers and at last she heard voices.

"Lady Lilian, can you hear me?"

"Lilian, please speak to me." Wet drops hit Lilian's face. Her sister was crying, it seemed. Whatever had happened to her, it must be bad.

She tried to open her eyes but could see naught but blackness. *I am so tired.*

"We heard a shot and then saw the horses. We came to help." A strong, masculine voice penetrated the fog in her head. *Who was this?* She could hear only snippets of the conversation because of the ringing in her ears.

"Lady Lilian, we must move you…"

"...gown ripped…"

"...back of gown wet with blood."

Are they talking about me?

Lilian felt herself being lifted and then coming to rest against a warm body. The horse shifted beneath them and was soothed with a soft murmur. She could smell the comforting aroma of its sweat, and shivered. Why was she so cold? She recognized her sister's voice, but her garbled words were disjointed.

A light scent of bay leaf and bergamot teased her nose. Gentlemen's and lady's colognes had been in abundance during her coming out, and had mostly tortured her senses, but this was one she liked. How odd that both scents were conveyed so distinctly. *Nothing was making sense. What was happening?* She felt helpless and trapped, now unable to see or hear, and fought against the urge to cry out. A rich voice above her calmed her trembling, and she found she could breathe. She could not hear what was being said, but the voice was soothing. Exhausted, Lilian leaned her head into the warm body holding her and gave in to the darkness that beckoned.

CHAPTER 1

London, England
Early August 1816

"Lilian, you look beautiful in Grandmama's antique pearls." Lydia, her twin, stood behind her and secured the clasp as Lilian stared at her reflection. "Grammy would want you to wear them when you meet your Prince Charming," her sister whispered, adding the matching pearl hair pins in her coiffure.

"Ouch!" Lilian gasped. "Do we have to wear these fripperies?" she challenged, struggling to keep the irritated tone from her voice. "Lydia, you promised not to ask this of me again, as long as I attended this ball—this *one* ball. I have your word." She slightly turned her head and met her sister's knowing smile. "Lydia, I *insist*. Promise me."

"Shall we just agree that I will not *badger* you? I may ask, though." Her sister grinned mischievously and darted to the door before turning back once more. "I will fetch our wraps and see how far on Mama is. She was close to being ready. *You know* she will expect us to set out the moment she comes down." Her twin flashed another mischievous grin towards Lilian and quickly left the room, pulling the door shut behind her.

Lilian sighed in frustration and glanced at the door through which her sister had just exited. Her sister meant well, but she wished Lydia would just accept her situation, just as she had done. She hated being dragged to social events and having to watch everything that she could no longer do, such as dancing. She winced at the loss. Dancing at these assemblies had been something she had always loved. She had dreamed about dancing with that special gentleman. Her mind could even summon up that one, special gentleman, not that it mattered. They had never officially met…*but that was before the accident—in the past.*

Her sister was undeterred in her mission to help Lilian walk again—so much so that every day her sister spent time lifting and massaging Lilian's lifeless legs. Lydia did not give a fig what others said. In her heart, she said, she knew her sister would walk again. Every day she worked Lilian's legs back and forth, up and down, and in a circular motion, moving them in a routine, convinced this would allow the muscles to stay intact for when her sister finally walked. Lilian touched her leg, hoping she would feel something. It was true. Her legs had not withered as so many had cautioned, they would.

Perhaps Lydia was right about this, she mused. *No.* As much as she wanted to believe, she could not. She shook her head. *Mayhap it is because we are twins and Lydia feels something will happen when I do not, but this is not guessing the colour of one's dress. She needs to realize that my legs will never work again.* Lilian dabbed away the quick tears from the corner of her eyes and smoothed her hands across her lap, freeing the wrinkles from her dress. She had accepted her circumstance and wished her twin could do the same. Life would be simpler.

A late burst of the evening sun shone through the window, rebounding off the cheval mirror and allowing Lilian to catch her reflection as she sat in the wheel-chair. It was ugly. The tall, hardwood slats of the back dwarfed her and made her look childlike in the centre. Clara had made her a pillow with goose down to help elevate her, but she still looked like a character in a fairy tale. Maybe she should be *Thumbelina,* she thought, unable to raise a smile. Even the carved edges of the black walnut made the vehicle look more imposing.

She sighed and touched the delicate Chantilly lace and pink satin bodice. At least she had a reason to wear one of her dresses from a year ago. Now she was crippled, she no longer belonged. *What does it matter what my dress looks like, since I can only grace the wallflowers?* This was her favourite dress and, secretly, she was glad to have occasion to wear it once more, although she would never tell Lydia that. Lilian loved the gown, which rested on her upper arms, revealing her shoulders. It boasted four layers of delicate lace and seed pearls over pale pink sarsnet and satin, which formed the bodice. A band of pale pink velvet hugged her upper waistline. The lace overdress hung past the bottom of the gown, giving it a flower-like appearance on the hem. She would never feel the lace flowing on the dance floor. With a huge sigh, she glanced at the Ormolu clock on the mantel, wishing she could move the hands and have this ball behind her.

"Lilian..." Lydia's excited voice reverberated up the stairs ahead of her footsteps, giving Lilian cause to laugh. Their mother would have an apoplectic fit. As her laughter grew, an unladylike snort escaped her. She could imagine her mother's reaction.

"We are ready to leave. Winston is here and will carry you downstairs to the coach. Your traveling chair is already attached."

Lilian winced at her sister's description of the traveling wheel-chair being tied to the back of the coach. The words rushed about her ears. *I hate this,* she thought bitterly. She heard nothing after *the chair,* and merely watched as Winston, the footman, stepped into the doorway. Lydia released the brake on Lilian's upstairs chair and wheeled her to the hall, where Winston scooped her from the wheel-chair and carried her down the stairs.

"There you are! Oh, my dears, you both look lovely." Her mother stood at the front entrance, already wearing her shawl and holding Lilian's over her arm. She looked at her butler. "Chambers, please inform my son that we are waiting for him to join us in the carriage."

"Certainly, your ladyship."

The Countess fussed about as Winston settled Lilian in the carriage and handed Lydia in beside her. At last she joined them, having delivered a list of unnecessary instructions.

"Ah! This is going to be such a wonderful night. I have both of my lovely daughters with me." She smiled in Lilian's direction. "My dear, I have no notion what your sister has said to convince you, but I am delighted you are joining us."

Lilian held her tongue. Her mother, like Lydia, completely ignored her useless legs and the wheel-chair that was now—embarrassingly—tied to the back of their carriage in full view. She wanted nothing more than to shrink beneath the seat she sat upon.

The whole night would be a test of stamina and courage. The thought that she would find her Prince Charming while sitting alongside the potted plants and wallflowers was preposterous. In fact, it was so ridiculous, she snorted out loud, as if she were still in the schoolroom.

"Did you say something, my dear?" her mother inquired in a voice of dangerous calm.

Lydia sniggered from across the carriage. Their mother glared at her.

"Lydia, I find that a very ill-bred sound. I shall have to discuss with your father the advisability of restricting your visits to the stables."

Lydia at once hung her head. "I am sorry, Mama. Please do not."

"Very well. Now, Lilian, what have you to say for yourself? You were not, I think, brought up in a sty?"

"No, Mama, of course not. I merely cleared my throat, I promise you. I apologize." It distressed her to discuss the matter any further. She knew better.

"Ah, the sun is making its final appearance, I see." In a swift change of mien, the Countess smiled at both girls. "This will be a wonderful evening, my daughters. Your father will join us there. He may already be there, waiting on us, although Robert is not usually ahead of me." Her mother smiled softly and then peered out of the window, still smiling. "We have always enjoyed these dances."

Indeed, her parents always danced together, even though the *ton* considered such niceties unfashionable. They were magical to watch when they waltzed, never seeming to care who looked upon them. Her parents were a love match—a rarity in the *ton*—nonetheless, it was what they wanted for their children. It was what Lilian had wanted too, *once upon a time,* before her accident. She had dreamed of being whisked away by love. Now, it was more akin to torture to recall those dreams. Instead, she read novels, as many as she could, diving into the lives of the heroes and heroines and relishing their good fortunes. This dance promised to be torture too.

Lost in her thoughts, she almost did not notice the cabriolet pull up, or her brother join them within.

"Good evening, lovely ladies. My apologies, Mama." Jonathan De Lacey dropped a kiss on his mother's cheek and sat down next to her. "I had a small matter to tie up with Father's man of business. It was important, or I would not have taken the time." He placed his hat in his lap as he spoke and pulled on his gloves.

Jonathan's affable nature always made her smile, Lilian mused. Always in a good mood, Jonathan invariably gave a warm smile, and offered to accompany his sisters on even the most mundane shopping trips.

An hour later, Lilian leaned back in a chair and fanned her face. The heat almost overwhelmed her. The ball was an absolute crush, even for those who, like her, sat by the wall. The hard-backed chair beneath her had already begun to fatigue her aching back. *I wish Lydia had not insisted. I cannot dance, not in a wheel-chair.* She glanced at her conveyance, placed discreetly behind a potted palm, a few chairs away. The pitying glances from the other mothers, and the hushed conversations of her childhood peers behind their fans, both upset and humiliated her.

Lilian watched her sister deftly handle the quadrille with a handsome blond soldier. Her mother was not likely to approve, but Lydia had a mind of her own, often seeing more of worth in a person than others did.

She laughed quietly to herself. That is why she was here, after all. Lydia had insisted she would meet the man of her dreams at a ball and had encouraged—no, forced—her to come to this ball. She heaved a sigh. Not one prince had acknowledged her, not that she had expected it.

A trickle of sweat ran down the front of her dress, while the cloying scents of competing perfumes abused her senses. Reaching into her reticule, Lilian withdrew her lace handkerchief and delicately touched it to her face, hoping the lilac cologne was still strong enough to last. She noticed many guests slipping out on to the veranda, which was the only place a little cool might be had and wished she might join them. A year ago, she had danced the quadrille until her feet blistered.

CHAPTER 2

She is here tonight! Lilian DeLacey. The beautiful young woman who had taken such a horrible spill from her horse a year ago, was here tonight. He would finally have a chance to meet her. He had inquired of her health each time he visited Lord Avalon, but it seemed both daughters had either been visiting with their mother or out shopping. This young lady had stolen his thoughts often over the past year, making him determined to meet her. If nothing else, it would put an end to the guilt he felt for her fall.

John Andrews, the fifth Earl of Harlow, sipped his champagne and studied the beauty across the ballroom. She looked a vision in the pink creation she wore. There had to be more to this picture, he reflected. It was not as if he could read women very well; however, he would not previously have pictured her as a wallflower. What, therefore, was she doing, sitting with the wallflowers? He looked around the room and spotted her sister on the dance floor with a fellow officer. Then he looked back at Lilian. Although she glanced at him, her eyes immediately darted away again. He followed her gaze to a table of potted ferns at the edge of the room and saw the object of her attention. A wheel-chair was just visible behind the fern.

"Can it be true?" he whispered to himself, feeling a mixture of surprise and sadness. Wheel-chairs were monstrous things. He remembered his grandfather had used one and they had not changed much since then. Lord Avalon would only say that his daughter had recovered as much as seemed possible. He had had no idea her recovery included that grotesque chair. A pang of sorrow gripped his heart. *Why did she affect him so?*

Harlow's gaze returned to her. A year ago, he and his best friend, Maxwell Wilde, the Earl of Worsley, had secured permission to use her father's lands in their search for an enemy of the Crown. A smuggling operation was rumoured to be happening from somewhere close to the edge of her father's property. The Earl of Avalon had given his permission for them to set up a look-out or do whatever was necessary to reconnoitre the area.

They had been on their way to the cliffs when a shot rang out. Crossing the road in front of them, a dark bay, ridden by a woman, raced out of control and ran down an embankment. Max and he galloped to catch up with the horse but were too late. They found Lilian DeLacey—Lady Lilian DeLacey—on the ground near a boulder. Her horse carried on running in the blind manner of frightened equines; although scared, it seemed to be unhurt and he had turned his attention to the girl. Seeing her sprawled on the hard earth, he thought the worst, until he found she was still breathing. It was shallow but steady and they returned her to her father. The poor man and his wife were deeply shaken. Only a short time earlier, that lady had mentioned both her daughters while they were taking tea with her. Neither of her daughters had appeared to meet Harlow and his friend as Lady Avalon had hoped. Now it was clear they had escaped the machinations of their mother in order to take a ride.

Returning to the present, Harlow was glad to see Lady Lilian DeLacey appearing much improved. She had been bruised and broken; however, he recalled the doctor examining her and telling her family he felt sure she had avoided injury to her spine and would walk again. *What had happened?*

Harlow walked towards a footman carrying the champagne and refreshed his drink, and then walked in her direction. Hearing pieces of conversation emanating from the group of older women ahead of him, he was suddenly reminded of his lack of formal introduction to Lady Lilian DeLacey. Deftly, he moved beyond the row of sitting debutantes towards a gaggle of hopeful mothers, amongst whom he recognized her mother.

"Good evening, Lady Avalon. Ladies." Effortlessly, he gave an elegant leg.

"Lord Harlow, a very good evening to you." Curtsying, the five women responded in unison, their turbaned heads covered in feathers and jewels that threatened to tip them over when they curtsied. Lady Avalon nodded, giving a practised smile and stepped forward, giving him her full attention.

Good God! The group of anxious mothers converged behind her, making him feel as one might if a piece of cooked mutton with forks poised to partake. He was no longer sure he wanted to meet anyone.

"I trust that you ladies are enjoying yourselves," he began, willing calmness to descend upon them.

"Truly, we are, my lord. And you? Are you enjoying yourself, as well, Lord Harlow?" Pointedly, Lady Avalon looked from him to her daughter on the dance floor. Smiling tightly, she invited him to follow her gaze. She seemed determined to bring her daughter to his notice, and he chided himself for what felt like a lapse in his own judgement. He should excuse himself now—he *wanted* to excuse himself. Unfortunately, the only way to meet Lilian was through her mother, at least for the moment.

"I am, indeed." He nodded and tossed a smile in the ladies' direction. "I wonder, Lady Avalon, if you would find it unseemly in me to ask for an introduction to your daughter? It occurred to me that I have never had the pleasure."

She smiled demurely, straining to look casually to her daughter on the dance floor.

"Certainly, Lord Harlow." She moved towards him, fairly gushing. "Your timing is impeccable. This dance is ending, although I feel certain she would enjoy your company…"

"Please." He held up his hand imploringly. "I apologize for the interruption, but you misunderstand, my lady. I am referring to your *other* daughter." He turned and nodded towards Lilian. She was still sitting with the other wallflowers, across the room from the dance floor, where her sister was just completing the final steps of a Cotillion, and away from the musical entertainment. Without reason, it pricked at his heart to see the young lady wearing a look of boredom and staring aimlessly at the dancers moving in front of her.

Startled, her mother glanced hesitantly in Lilian's direction and back to him, in a clear moment of bewilderment, before smoothly responding.

"Yes, of course, Lord Harlow. Please follow me." The two approached the row of wallflowers. Her daughter's bored countenance was fixed on the door to the veranda, and she did not notice their approach.

"Lilian…" Lady Avalon leaned forward and gently touched her daughter's shoulder, gaining her attention.

"Oh, Mama, please forgive my impertinence. I did not see you."

The Countess smiled broadly at her daughter. "My dear,

please allow me to make known to you Lord Harlow, an associate of your father's."

Harlow noticed a sudden change in the older woman's eyes, as if recognition dawned as she spoke.

"You must remember Lord Harlow. He was the gentleman who rescued you a year ago and returned you to us after your fall," she continued smoothly without waiting for Lilian's response. "Lord Harlow, please allow me to introduce my beautiful daughter, Lady Lilian DeLacey.

Harlow winced, comprehending the flicker of pain which crossed Lilian's face at the mention of the accident. Nevertheless, he mused, from a wholly selfish point of view it gave him leave to ask questions of the accident and for that he was grateful.

He flashed a warm smile at her anxious face and bowed gallantly. "Lady Lilian, I thought I recognized you and your sister when I arrived. Two such beauties always light up a room."

She nodded at his words, her expression one of torment.

I understand that emotion, he thought to himself. "This chair would appear not to be taken. I wonder if you would mind if I sat next to you for a few moments?" He struggled to order his thoughts as he spoke. He did not want to embarrass her by asking her to dance or take a turn when she had obviously gone to some lengths to avoid her wheel-chair. He wanted to become acquainted with her, but he knew he must be cautious. It was a dilemma indeed.

"Lord Harlow, I am most pleased to make your acquaintance," she responded tentatively, her voice low. "However, the seats are all..." She broke off, looking from side to side, and appeared, for the first time, to notice the two vacant seats to her right. A glimmer of amusement lit up her eyes. "The seats do appear to be empty," she finished, with a slight smile and touched the unoccupied seat.

Harlow permitted himself a slight smile. He had observed two young women vacating their seats and walking in the direction of the supper room a few minutes before. Lady Lilian had been looking in the opposite direction at the time. The ladies had still not returned. Perhaps they were on the dance floor. However, that might be, it was fortuitous for him. They could have a short conversation. *I will make it be enough.*

"Surely your kindness may indulge me, if only for a few moments?" he coaxed, his blue eyes twinkling.

"Well, if that is settled, I will leave you two to talk." Lady Avalon glanced at her daughter and displayed a hopeful smile before returning to her friends.

"Lady Lilian, I had hoped, one day, to meet you formally. You should know I have inquired of your health several times." He kept his own voice low. "I would, however, with your permission, like to ask you a question."

She nervously glanced towards her chair. "That is kind, Lord Harlow, but..."

Sensing her embarrassment, he quickly added, "I wondered if I might call on you tomorrow and take you for a drive."

"Lord Harlow, I..." Lilian flushed and glanced away for a moment. "You are most generous, my lord..."

Her eyes spoke of intelligence. "Lady Lilian, if you are worried about your wheel-chair, I have seen it and that matters not to me. Your company is what matters." He smiled broadly. "If you are amenable to my attentions, I will call on you tomorrow morning and take you for a drive about the park." He did not want to be turned down. For some inexplicable reason, he felt drawn to the girl. Over the past year, her broken image had sporadically flooded his mind for no obvious reason. To see her seated among the wallflowers, as if on the row of shame, unnerved him.

"I...yes, I would be honoured, my lord." A look of relief flashed across her face, ahead of a speculative smile.

"Shall we say ten of the clock?" The current dance ended, and two young ladies dressed in white satin, on the arms of escorts and bubbling with excitement, returned to their seats in time to hear his offer to call. Their animation was audible, causing Lilian to blush.

She nodded her assent. "I look forward to it, my lord," she added.

It was done. Perhaps a day in her company would solve the feelings he had had this past year. It could only be a fascination. Once he had met with her and spent time in her company, he felt certain the dreams would leave. He was only concerned for her safety, after all. His conscience wrestled with what had occurred. The accident had cut her down, an innocent young lady, and he felt somewhat responsible, even if he had arrived in time to help her. However, something else troubled him. What if he actually developed deeper feelings for this girl?

Harlow needed some fresh air. He had had enough of this dreary ball and asked a footman to retrieve his cloak. Lilian Delacey seemed nothing like her brother, Jonathan, Viscount DeLacey, whose arrogance grated on his nerves. They had all been friends in school until DeLacey joined a group of boys overly obsessed with their positions in society, who frequently tried to make those beneath them the butt of jokes. *Mother nagged me into coming,* he grumbled to himself. *However, seeing Lilian DeLacey has made the evening worthwhile.* His purpose for attending unexpectedly fulfilled, he felt no further need to be here.

Secure in his coach, he settled comfortably into the red leather squabs and rested his feet on the seat in front of him, trying to clear his mind. Despite his best efforts, however, meeting Lady Lilian took his thoughts back to the day of the accident, a day he recalled vividly.

He and Max Wilde had just gained Lord Avalon's assistance in curtailing the source of increasing smuggling in the area. Tintagel's close proximity to Cornwall was noteworthy, and a survivor from a recent wrecked ship—allegedly pirated by locals—had managed to get word to Customs and Excise of rumours swirling about a location in Tintagel. The description was nebulous, but pointed to a well-known public house, one run by a woman and her brother. The smuggling seemed concentrated on ships known to carry silks, brandy and spices. There were several taverns in Tintagel, and they suspected that the DeLacey land held a piece of the puzzle, for Avalon's property ran down to the cliffs. The two men had been in the area for a few days, exploring the town and trying to smoke out any undercurrents of smuggling activity.

Harlow had been surprised to learn of Avalon's ties to his own commanding officer, Lieutenant-General Martin DeLacey. He had suggested they ride out to meet his cousin and gain his assistance. Their new dealings were to be explained as a venture with the East India Company, if others asked. The meeting with Lord Avalon had been as anticipated. He had told them he would meet with his man of business and set up an account to establish legitimacy, should there be any question. Having concluded business with Lord Avalon, they were heading back to their lodgings in town when the accident happened.

The road the men travelled ran below a beautiful ridge. Laughter drew Harlow's attention to the two young ladies above, both riding like the wind. Unbound, their dark hair flowed like water in the breeze, while the teasing sounds of their girlish chuckles called to him. An older groom trailed behind them and it appeared that they were deliberately outmanoeuvring the poor fellow. Harlow at once recognized the girls, being one who prided himself on never forgetting a face. They were the Earl's twin daughters; he had noticed them at a recent London ball. He had been charmed by both of them, but the one in the sapphire gown had immediately drawn his interest. Their eyes had met when he entered the room, even though he had made no move to meet her.

Harlow had no interest in the marriage mart. Nevertheless, he continually dreamed and the moments surrounding Lady Lilian's accident haunted his sleep still, joining other nightmares from the war which also plagued him. Whenever she came to mind, usually during his dreams, he relived that scene. She was riding a horse, there was a shot and she was thrown from her mount, then to slide and roll over a dozen or more protruding rocks. The same dream repeated itself over and over, making him wake up in a cold sweat. *What was so special about this lady?*

His mother had continually attempted to cajole him into finding a lady to marry so she could have grandchildren, even going so far as to trick him into meetings with the latest debutante beauty. He had resisted. It was not that he did not wish to marry, but what woman would want to have a man who screamed in terror during the night?

He had admired Lilian's and her sister's pluck that fateful day. Avalon's wife had planned to introduce her daughters and had had the audacity to invite both Max and him to join her in the parlour when her husband's meeting ended. He chuckled, thinking about the empty parlour. The girls had escaped, taking to their horses before she could gain their attendance. Although Lady Avalon did not seem one to let her temper get the better of her, the tight-lipped smile the Countess had worn while she made small talk and served tea to them both had told him there would be more to come. This mother had planned a reckoning with her daughters.

Harlow appreciated a woman with a streak of independence, although that could not be said of many of his friends. When he spotted Avalon's daughters galloping neck and neck along the ridge that day, he was further intrigued. Both horses reared at the sudden shot. Max's and his horses neighed in alarm but were more accustomed, due to service in the war, to loud noises, and the men were able to maintain control. The girl in the blue habit lost her seat and disappeared from his view.

The shot sounded close, as if it had come from his left. Luckily the bullet missed them all. However, since that fateful day he had often wondered if the shot had been accidental? *Had the bullet been meant for them?*

CHAPTER 3

Lilian had seen the handsome gentleman glance her way more than once and always with a heart-melting smile. She tried her best not to stare in his direction, yet found her eyes drawn to him, nonetheless. As dancers swished their way across the floor, she strained to catch sight of him from the corner of her eye and made small excuses to herself each time she realized what she was doing. Seeking her mother's whereabouts was the last excuse she offered, a ridiculous pretence quite unworthy of her intelligence.

Mama had not left the side of the hostess, Lady Smyth, and her friends since she had returned to them following Lilian's own introduction to Lord Harlow, barely an hour ago. What was even more distressing, each time she looked in her mother's direction, Mama and her friends were looking in hers, forcing her to give what Mama referred to as her *pretend smile*. No matter, she justified, it would have to do since she was not interested in being here. Well, she thought, with a tiny twitch of her lips, she had not been until an hour ago.

If she had not become such a cynic this past year, she

would have believed—no, she would have wished—John Andrews to be her Prince Charming. Indeed, he looked every bit the gentleman she would have imagined. His thick, wavy brown hair hung to the top of his collar, framing a square, dimpled chin. His broad shoulders accentuated a smaller waist, drawing her attention to his very athletic body. He stood taller than many of the men in the room, a quality that, as she perused his body from the vantage of her chair, looked imposing.

A flash of red caused her to look in his direction. *Is he leaving?* Quickly, she turned her head away from him, in case he looked back, and realized she had barely noticed anything or anyone other than *him* since she had made his acquaintance. She shook her head, summoning the will to think of anything else except his sparkling blue eyes and the smile that warmed her to her toes whenever he flashed it in her direction. *Think of...anything but him,* she ordered herself. Lilian squeezed her eyes shut for a moment, hoping she would see something different when she opened them.

This cannot be happening. She groaned inwardly. Lord Harlow's red uniform was too easy to spot, and she watched him make his way towards the front of the room, stopping to speak with the hostess, her two daughters, and Lilian's own mother. A woman dressed in a red satin and gold gown, with reddish-blonde hair in an elaborately jewelled chignon, sauntered from behind him and hastily placed her gloved hand on his arm. She must have said something to the other women, because they immediately stepped back from Lord Harlow, and walked away, whispering. *How will I ask Mama about her without it becoming a point of discussion with her?* Lilian allowed herself to think about that, certain her mother had information, while she studied the correlation between them all from her safe vantage point; watching their body movements with keen interest. She was becoming adept at predicting people's moods by watching their body and their expressions. The wheel-chair provided plenty of opportunity for her to perfect this skill.

Who is that woman? After a few minutes, Lord Harlow leaned in the woman's direction and whispered...something. The woman pulled back, laughed and swatted his arm with her fan, but the scene seemed wrong—almost forced. The woman tapped his arm once again and nodded, almost imperceptibly, before she strolled towards a man standing by the refreshment table. *Did she and Lord Harlow plan a later assignation?* A strange feeling hit the pit of Lilian's stomach and warmth shot up her neck. *Was that jealousy? Impossible!* She used the notebook in her reticule to fan her face before remembering her delicate white lace satin fan was hanging from her arm. She whipped open the folds, moving the object quickly to create a breeze across the sudden moistness on her face and neck. Scanning the room, Lilian spotted the open door to the terrace, wishing herself out there. Hundreds of beeswax candles had warmed the room miserably, and the dark pink colour of the walls added to a morbid fear of being closed into a small space.

Peering through the dancers, Lilian spotted her sister twirling about, now waltzing with Lord Richard Yarstone. Her soft, peach silk dress gently wrapped the sides of her legs as they twirled, her golden slippers protruding ever so subtly from beneath. Lord Yarstone was naught if not persistent where Lydia was concerned. Lilian thought they reciprocated each other's feelings. *And,* if she counted correctly, that was the second dance for them—together. She smiled to herself. *They* might not be counting, however, it was a certainty Mama was doing so. She tallied everything, unfortunately.

Lord Yarstone would arrive promptly at ten of the clock. She expected the front parlour would be lined with white roses tomorrow, his usual choice. White roses signified new beginnings and everlasting love. It was everything that Lydia deserved.

A wistful sigh escaped Lilian, causing her to clap her hand to her mouth and look around, embarrassed. The surrounding girls were absorbed in conversation and had not seemed to notice her. That was part of the problem—she felt unworthy of notice. Lydia's acquaintance with Lord Yarstone was becoming more serious. It was what she wanted, and Lilian was pleased for her sister. However, this only added to the lacklustre feeling which had crept over her of late about her own life, sitting here with naught except an oversized wheel-chair as her steady companion. Her sister, her best friend, would marry and leave home, separating them for the first time in their lives.

Suddenly feeling rather overwhelmed, Lilian was ready to leave. She had promised to come, and she had fulfilled her part of the bargain. She hung her head, as much for shame as despair at her thoughts. She was so lost in her thoughts she failed to see her sister and Lord Yarstone approaching.

"Are you ready to depart, Lilian?" Lydia's eyes crinkled at the corners with mirth.

Already? "Truly?" *Lydia is ready to leave? Unheard of.* She subtly turned to the door in time to see Lord Harlow exit the ballroom, and a quiver ran up her arm. It was hard to be unaffected by his dashing presence, particularly so when he wore his crisp, red uniform. "Yes, Lydia, if you are prepared." She smiled weakly, keeping her enthusiasm at bay on purpose. "It is a little warm on this side of the room, especially since there are no exits." She gave a few more flaps of the fan, as if to emphasize her point, before putting it away.

"I agree, it is rather warm."

"Lady Lilian, may I fetch your chair for you?" Lord Yarstone inquired.

Containing a sly smile, she nodded and watched him retrieve her chair from behind the small arch of potted plants. The plants were delicately intertwined to affect a small garden of greenery that curved to embellish the corner of the room. *Besotted* was the word Father had used when describing Lord Yarstone.

"You must tell me all," Lydia whispered softly, grinning. "I saw *him* talking to you." She emphasized the word *him.* "And do not pretend you do not know of whom I am speaking, sister."

Pretending not to know what she was speaking of made little sense. Her sister would be sure to wheedle out the story in no time. Feeling impish, however, Lilian determined to make Lydia wriggle a little first. "It was naught save a momentary conversation," she said at last. A curious feeling of satisfaction rippled through her. Yet, when she looked back at Lydia, she saw her sister's smirk of satisfaction. Blood rushed from her neck to her temples; she felt its heat. *I cannot hide anything from her.*

"Surely, 'twas not just a conversation. It was deliberate, purposeful. I insist you tell me everything! That was Lord Harlow. Every debutante in the room had her eyes on you when he walked in your direction," her sister whispered. "Your Prince Charming!" Her head bobbed slightly with happiness. "And you stalked him afterwards. Do not try to deny it; I saw you."

"Do not be silly. How could I do such a thing when I am tied to a chair?" *They caught me!*

"You still have eyes, dearest."

"Lydia, may we please discuss this in the carriage?" Lilian pleaded softly, her face beginning to burn. She heard rustling and turned her head to see all the wallflowers, heedless of good manners, were craning their necks in her direction.

Lord Yarstone cleared his throat. "My ladies, your mother

has seen us and appears to be saying her goodbyes. Would it be permissible to escort you to the door?"

"Thank you, Lord Yarstone. We would appreciate that greatly." Lydia smiled and moved in front of her sister's chair.

Lilian lifted her arms and allowed Lydia to pull her to a standing position as Lord Yarstone exchanged the chairs behind her, allowing her to settle into the wheel-chair. *I hate this part. It is humiliating.* She mustered a faint smile, a false smile, but a smile all the same. She would not give them anything to talk about *on purpose*. She could only imagine the number of people watching the awkward exit. Lydia claimed she would walk again, pointing out her ability to stand. Frankly, Lilian understood none of it. She felt trapped in this chair. Lord Yarstone waited until she was seated and then escorted their small party to their carriage.

A little over an hour later, the girls were back at their father's town house, in their suite of rooms. Lilian liked the fact that Father and Mama had made their rooms into adjoining apartments. Each had their own bedroom with a small retiring area attached, joined together by a larger private parlour. As children, this room lent itself as a small nursery or room for their nurse, should their health demand it. Lilian's rooms were in subtle tones of blues while her sister's rooms were pink.

"Lilian, once I have changed my gown, I will come back. Do not expect me not to beg for all the details. You must tell me."

"Really, Lydia...there is little to say," Lilian responded.

"Nonsense. Do not prevaricate. There is much to comment on. I *watched* you." Triumph gleamed in her eyes. "I only wish the steps of the dance would have brought us closer to where you were sitting, so I would not have to wait."

Lilian winced. "You would not have heard a thing. The

music was loud," she murmured. "Besides, since we are on the subject, I noticed Lord Yarstone's particular attentions towards you. Mayhap we should place bets on what type of flower he will send tomorrow. He must get up very early, as I think on it, to buy all the white roses in Town.

"White roses are lovely and convey such beautiful messages. Do you remember the halls full of flowers we had last year?" Lilian reflected, musing aloud about the bouquets the two of them had received the previous Season.

"And *you* will soon have flowers again, my beautiful sister," Lydia retorted. "Heed my words," she added in a prophetic tone.

"I love the roses he brings you. I cannot wait to see what tomorrow brings," Lilian murmured, as much to herself as to her sister.

"I hope 'tis nothing too romantic. I am not sure I want to commit myself to any gentleman this early in the Season." Lydia's voice trailed after her as she left the room—leaving Lilian to her thoughts.

The door to her bedchamber opened again and Clara entered, followed by two younger housemaids carrying water and a tray. She stoked the fire and then addressed the two underlings.

"Abby, do fill the basin with fresh water, please? Mary, my girl, put the camomile tea and biscuits on the table next to Lady Lilian's bed if you will." The maids did as bid and left. Clara was always very respectful in her dealings with the other maids. The servants all loved her—the women, especially because of her many kindnesses towards them. Every Christmas, she added a small box of treats to their gift, usually ribbons, which she had purchased with her own money throughout the year and tucked away for the festivity.

"My lady, how did you enjoy the ball?" Clara made quick work of removing Lilian's hair pins and jewellery, carefully tucking her grandmother's pearls back into the jewellery case.

"It was lovely. Greenery formed delicate corner arches that gave the impression that the room was rounded. The pale wooden floors shown like mirrors under the light of hundreds of beeswax candles. It was a crush and quite warm." Lilian tried to describe the room, but all she could think about was a tall, handsome soldier in his dashing red uniform.

She efficiently unlaced the back of Lilian's dress and lifted it over her head.

"I can brush out my hair, Clara. You have so much to do after these affairs, especially now."

"Nonsense, m'lady. It is my great pleasure to see to both of my beautiful girls. What I would nay give to be a fly on the wall to hear the accounts of this evening, seeing the smiles the both of ye are wearing."

"Saucebox!" Lilian playfully admonished her childhood nurse. The twins' relationship with Clara had grown close over the years and she never hesitated to voice her opinion, a habit Mama abhorred. However, being accustomed to Clara's forthright ways, Lydia and Lilian would think it odd if she did not speak her mind, so much like a second mother had she become.

"I heard ye had a gentleman ask for an introduction." The older woman clicked her tongue softly and smiled.

"Who told you?" Lilian's face heated. "I have not even discussed it with Lydia. Yes, Lord Harlow asked Mama to make me known to him."

"Oh, the gentleman who saved your life? A true prince, to be sure. He is a good-looking chap! I declare, I should be mighty glad to receive him. Asked to meet you, did he?" Clara's eyes twinkled. "I have heard he has asked after you each time he visits your father."

Servants always talk. Yet who could have told her so soon? Mama! Lilian should know better than to be surprised.

"Clara, I shall tell Lydia in a few moments. Indeed, I shall receive no sleep otherwise."

Clara tittered. "'Tis enough to know there is more, m'lady. I shall be away to your sister, for I fear she will be fit to burst, waiting to hear all about it." She gently chucked her charge under the chin and scurried off to help Lydia, leaving Lilian feeling a myriad emotions. She was excited—and it scared her. To be sure, she had met with many young gentlemen…however, that had been *last year*. Not since she had had her accident, and been confined to a wheel-chair, had she entertained gentlemen callers. She was not sure she had the stomach for it. Moving her chair close to her bed, she locked the brake and transferred herself to her bed, something she found doable using the strength of her arms.

"I can see that you are trying to wriggle out of whatever wonderful thing is about to happen, and I will not allow it, little sister!" Lydia cheerfully bounded into the room in her usual hoydenish fashion and jumped on the bed beside her. "Tell me everything!"

"*Little sister?* We are the same age!" Lilian playfully swatted at her twin. "You know quite well I am the elder…"

"By mere seconds. You took your time in greeting the world too, I will add. In fact, according to Mama, I chased you out! I was directly on your heels." Lydia's voice was full of cheer.

"I am ready to tell all." As she recounted her time with Lord Harlow, she realized that she had a much better evening than she had imagined and looked forward to seeing him again.

"That cannot be all. I must hear everything. Hurry!" Lydia prodded gently. As she spoke, Lydia put her finger up and they stopped talking long enough to listen for anyone walking outside in the hall, making sure their mother had not heard their comments. She had a way of creeping up on them. When convinced her mother was nowhere near, Lydia continued, "Practice your *fractious* face. As you know, Mama can go from being gleeful to—figuratively at least—skewering a person in a heartbeat when crossed," she said.

They dearly loved their mother but her overbearing presence of late had become difficult. Indulging an occasional, private joke was their only comic relief. Perhaps it was her way of dealing with Lilian's disability. Whatever had provoked it, Mama had become fierce in her drive to find matches for both her daughters, and seemed to forget that she had, at one time, encouraged their marrying for love. Lilian realized that most of this effort was because of her injuries.

"Come on, then, blow the gab."

"I beg your pardon?" Lilian feigned surprise, although the slang term was familiar from the many hours they had spent in the stables.

"Tell me. What did he say? I saw him sit next to you and speak. I stepped on poor Yarstone's foot when Lord Harlow sat down."

Lilian beamed. Of all things, she wanted to tell Lydia. "Oh, very well!" She threw up her hands in a show of mock surrender. "He walked over to me with Mama. She introduced him and then left reluctantly. I could tell she wished to stay. It is my belief he asked Mama to introduce him." Lilian felt her grin stretch until it took up so much of her face it hurt. Closing her eyes, she summoned his image. She had tried for months to recall the man who had rescued her. Lydia had described him as handsome; even now, Lilian could not recall his features from a year ago. What she remembered was his scent. It was the same fragrance which had assailed her tonight. "He asked me to go for a drive tomorrow."

"Really? That is marvellous!" Lydia jumped up and down and clapped her hands furiously. "I am so happy for you, my sweet sister."

"What are you happy for, my dear?" The door opened and her mother walked in with a maid following behind her, carrying a tray. "I know you have had a tea tray. I thought, perhaps, a small cup of chocolate would make the night more restful."

"Mama, that is so thoughtful. You *know* how I love chocolate." Lydia reached for the cup.

"What were you girls talking about just now? Why are you so happy, my dear?" Mama looked at Lydia.

"Mama," the words gushed from Lydia's mouth as water from a pump. "Lord Harlow has asked to take my darling sister for a drive tomorrow. I think he means to court her."

"Lydia!" Lilian flushed.

"Well, my dears, it seems tonight was a success for both my daughters." She sat between them and hugged them to her, then looked at Lilian.

"Please, Mama," Lilian pleaded. "Please do not expect anything to become of his attentions. He is just being solicitous and wished to meet me to assure himself of my good health."

"Nonsense. That man has been wanting to meet you for a year. Your father has mentioned that Lord Harlow has inquired often, mostly through a messenger, of your health. I am hopeful for both of you." She kissed first Lilian and then Lydia on the top of the head before leaving the room.

"I think Mama does know best, this time." Lydia squeezed Lilian's hand. "I am for my bed. Good night, dearest." So saying, she also departed.

Lilian lay and watched the candlelight dance effortlessly

on the soft blue and white printed wallpaper of her room. Feeling her eyes about to close, she forced herself to sit up and blow out the candle on the walnut night-table and then, lay back and smoothed the covers over herself. Her curtains were slightly apart and allowed a sliver of moonlight to enter. She stared at the light on the ceiling, imagining it as starlight. Shutting her eyes tight, she made a small wish. Tonight, she asked the stars that her mother would be right. Tonight, every part of Lilian hoped it could be true.

CHAPTER 4

The next morning, Harlow whistled in the crisp morning air as he drove the short distance to Lord Avalon's Mayfair town house. The weather had cooperated, his neckcloth did not pinch, and Cook had provided his favourite dishes for breakfast. Everything was right with the world. And, most important of all, he would see the woman who had occupied so many of his dreams of late—in a matter of minutes.

He was so caught up in his musings, he nearly missed the furious sounds of horses running down the street. Looking up, he spotted a black coach drawn by black horses hurtling in his direction, its driver yelling at the terrified horses, which appeared to have bolted. With only a moment to spare, Harlow whipped up his pair and swung his yellow curricle to the side of the road, as the black coach sped past him, leaving a cloud of dust in its wake. "Are you alright, Simmons, he yelled to his tiger, who had been in the small box seat at the back.

"Ye...yes, m'lord. I believe I am," a shaking voice replied.

"'Tis a testament to your skills, m'lord," he added in a strained voice.

"I am debating whether we should disembark and kiss the ground before proceeding," Harlow joked.

"I thought we were going to do exactly that, m'lord," the tiger retorted, unflinchingly.

"Ha! Simmons, you have right of it!" Good humouredly, Harlow held the reins in one hand, and pulled off his hat, blowing off the dust that covered it.

"Well, boys," he muttered aloud to his chestnuts, "'Tis a good job the bloke regained control of his horses before they ran over someone. Come to think of it, I do not recall ever seeing a coach racket through this part of Town before. Mayhap he has an appointment with the devil himself." Recollecting that he wished to keep his good mood, he shook the remaining dust from his hat, rolled it around to make sure the shape was correct and placed it back on his head. "That could have had unfortunate consequences had there been people in the street."

Slowly turning his horses, he nonchalantly tried to observe any movement in the alley as he tooled quietly back the way he had come, Harlow noticed that the black coach had slowed down and pulled off the main street into an alley. *Odd, that,* he thought. He circled the block and peered through the alley. He saw nothing moving except the heads of what appeared to be the same horses which had just passed him. The horses' heads were tossing back and forth in some irritation, white flecks of foam spotting their forelegs. The vehicle and the animals' hindquarters were hidden behind a well-respected public house.

"Very odd place to park a coach…unless someone has died in the tap," he mumbled to himself, making a mental note to discuss this oddity with his friend Max. Satisfied with his resolve, he turned about again, signalled his horses to pick up speed and, ten minutes later, pulled his curricle into the circular drive to Avalon House on Norfolk Street.

The beautiful, combined grey stone and pink brick mansion stood three storeys tall and was surrounded by black iron railings. Window boxes filled with flowers known for their fragrance hugged the sills of several upstairs windows, while white and pink rose bushes dominated the gardens that framed the house. The soft fragrance of roses floated on the light breeze, welcoming Harlow and reminding him of the flowers he had brought as he handed the reins to his tiger. He reached for the bouquet of purple forget-me-nots, kept safely in a hidden box behind his feet.

A moment passed, and the door opened. "Good morning, my lord." The butler stepped back, allowing entry, and held his hand out to receive Harlow's hat and gloves. "Shall I take the flowers for you, Lord Harlow?"

Harlow shifted the bouquet as he removed his gloves, handing both them and his hat to the butler.

"Thank you, Chambers, but I would like to give them to Lady Lilian myself."

"Of course, my lord. Please follow me."

Harlow thought he caught a faint smile cross the old retainer's face before it disappeared, as if he was pleased for Lady Lilian. Harlow's heart warmed.

The door to the parlour opened before Chambers could knock and a young lady rushed through the door, her attention still on a person behind her in the room. She slid to a stop, just short of toppling the old man, who had already begun protective measures, stepping against the wall and holding out his hands.

"Oh, good gracious. Please accept my apology, sir. I thought Lord Yarstone..." She stopped in mid-sentence; a smile crept up her face and she gave a quick curtsy. "Lord

Harlow, do forgive me." The smile lit her face. "I expect you have come to see my sister, Lilian."

"I have, indeed." He smiled pleasantly. The girl looked almost identical to her sister, except for the slate blue colour of her eyes, a contrast to her sister's deeper, blue-green. Lady Lydia's reddish-brown hair had been gathered into a modest knot, framed by curls and small white flowers. "Beg pardon for staring, but this is the first time I have seen the two of you so close together. You are almost identical twins!" Harlow felt a fool as soon as he made the observation out loud.

"Yes, my lord, we are, and I am afraid we filled our childhood with pranks. She smiled mischievously and nodded toward her sister. "Those around us tried to make us look different in our dress, a tactic I fear we…ah…put to good use."

"Lady Lydia, please accept my apologies." The voice of the butler interrupted any further indiscreet confidences. The old man had recovered his wits and his balance.

"Chambers, it is I who should apologize. I am at fault, not you." Lady Lydia stepped aside to allow him entry into the parlour and quickly moved to stand behind a winged-back chair near her sister. "Lilian, I believe Lord Yarstone has just arrived." While Lady Lydia's voice was almost a whisper, she could not refrain from smiling widely. "Would you mind if we also took a turn in the park? He said he would bring his phaeton."

"Oh, gracious! Lydia, please…daughter, your manners!" The Countess blustered into the room with evident frustration and gave a piercing look in the direction of her errant child. "Lord Harlow, what a pleasant surprise this is." Her voice was at once calm and even.

He extended his leg and gave a slight bow.

"An excursion as you describe would be most pleasant, I

am sure, ladies," Harlow interposed. He could not help hearing Lady Lydia's whispered request.

The room offered a bright and cheery respite from the world, and Harlow imagined they must use it more than just when they received guests. A soft yellow and blue damask wallpaper covered the walls. Light blue velvet curtains framed the front window, hanging over thin curtains. The delicate fabric beckoned light into the room. A deep blue velvet settee with walnut edging sat against the far wall, and a yellow and white striped winged-back chair stood in a slight, diagonal angle from the wall opposite the door. Resting on a small, adjacent wooden table was a vase of potted greenery. To his left, near the door, a tall walnut secretaire, with colourful leather-bound books lining two upper shelves, stood sentry against the wall.

Looking beyond the twin sister and her mother, Harlow spotted his quarry sitting in her chair near an over-large window, holding a small blue book which she had evidently been reading. Lady Lilian placed her book in her lap and looked up at him, smiling shyly.

His mouth ran dry and he suddenly felt as if he had stuffed it with cotton. He tried to swallow and clear it; coughing instead, he was left feeling very much like a tongue-tied schoolboy of twelve. Unnerved, he thrust the handful of forget-me-nots in front of him, wiping with his free hand at sudden moisture that had formed over his brow. *This is a new occurrence. When has giving flowers to any woman ever made me nervous? I have never been at a loss for words. This woman—the woman who has haunted my dreams—appears to have affected all cogent parts of my being. Tomfool!* Despite the inner turmoil, he pressed forward.

"These are for you, Lady Lilian."

"My lord, what lovely flowers!" Her hands gripped the wheels of her chair to move them.

"Lilian…please, my dear, allow me to help you." Her mother stood up and moved towards Lady Lilian, and released the brake on the chair, pushing it closer to the parlour couch.

Lady Lilian relaxed her arm. Harlow stepped closer, continuing to chastise himself for acting like an idiot.

"Thank you, Mama," Lady Lilian replied. She accepted the flowers from Harlow, and lifting them to her nose, inhaled deeply. "Thank you, sir. They are a favourite of mine. They smell lovely.

A deep voice sounded from behind him. "Lord Yarstone, my lady."

"Please show him…in…" Lady Lydia's voice faltered. Glancing up, Harlow was in time to see the withering look she received from her mother.

"Thank you, Chambers," Lady Avalon answered tersely. Harlow recalled seeing his father deliver a similar look, once upon a time, and swallowed, suddenly feeling sympathy for Lydia.

"Lord Harlow, I had not expected to see you." Richard, Viscount Yarstone, stiffened and slowly withdrew a large bunch of white roses from behind his back.

"Relax," Harlow uttered under his breath. Yarstone appeared slightly more irritated each time they met near the DeLacey sisters. Clearing his throat, he said aloud, "Lady Lilian, are you still amenable to a drive in the park?"

Lilian nodded. "I should be pleased to accompany you, sir, if…" She looked up at her mother. "Mama?"

"Lord Harlow, of course, nothing could be more acceptable." The Countess beamed. "Do not forget your pelisse, my dear. There is a slight chill in the air today," she added, accepting the flowers from Lilian.

"Lady Lydia, these are for you," Yarstone spoke, holding out his spray to Lilian's twin.

"Oh my, white roses! They are so beautiful." Lady Lydia sniffed them and smiled at the Viscount.

"Lady Lydia, it is a pleasant day. I was hoping...would you care to join me for a ride in my phaeton?" Lord Yarstone shifted on his feet, seemingly nervous.

The Countess did not wait for her daughter to answer. "She would indeed, sir. You are very kind to so indulge her. You gentlemen have chosen a beautiful day for a turn about the park." She accepted Lydia's flowers and cast a quick look at Lilian.

"Do try not to get into trouble, my dears," she chided gently.

Harlow caught the look of hope in Lady Avalon's eyes. He could only imagine the strain that the family had been under these past many months. A pang of guilt attacked his heart. He still had not determined the origin of the shot which had caused the accident and try as he might, could not shake the fear that his earlier inquiries in Tintagel connected him to this tragedy.

"We will return in two hours, my lady." he offered.

The Countess looked warily at him. "A footman will assist Lady Lilian into the carriage, sir." She tugged on a rope near the settee. A knock on the door quickly followed it and Winston entered on his mistress' command.

"It appears we shall have a beautiful day together. Shall we adjourn to the park, ladies?" Lord Yarstone held the parlour door open for the group to depart, a look of unbridled delight in his eyes. He held out his arm to Lydia, and the two of them led the small group to the phaeton and curricle waiting outside.

"Wait! Cook sent this for you, m'ladies." Clara came scurrying behind them with another maid, each carrying a picnic basket and a blanket. "In case you become hungry," she added, smiling at the two young ladies.

"Thank you for your thoughtfulness, Clara," Lilian said kindly. "Lord Harlow, Clara is our maid."

Harlow nodded. "That was very nice of you, Clara."

"Now, be off with you or the day will be done afore you get there!" Clara adjoined, waving to the four of them as they pulled away from the house.

I will let nothing mar this day, Harlow thought to himself. His stomach contracted when he glanced at the beautiful woman sitting beside him, and he allowed a small smile to shape his mouth. His mother would be pleased, and he should be happy, and he would be, if he could quell the agitation he felt roiling in the pit of his stomach.

CHAPTER 5

It was a wonderful day for a picnic in Richmond Park. Except for a few words about perhaps partaking of a picnic together, the foursome agreed to join forces and enjoy the scenery in tandem. Except for minimal pleasantries, conversation between Lilian and Harlow faded into a comfortable silence as they enjoyed the park.

There was only the slightest chill in the air, but this year the weather seemed a little cooler than normal. Considering the extreme cold of last winter, when the Thames froze hard enough for an elephant to walk across—at least that was what she had been told—it could not surprise her. Ordinary folk were out walking, reading books under trees, and eating lunches, without the perpetual, inconvenient rain or the heat of the summer.

Lilian snuggled into her lightweight pelisse. She wished Mama had not made such a fuss about her taking a wrap. She felt Lord Harlow might then have lent her his coat, something she felt sure would have warmed her clear to her toes. Thanks to Mama, she was left to warm herself.

It was a time to see and be seen. Almost a year had passed

since her last such carriage ride through park, and it had been Hyde Park. Life had been different, then. Lydia and Lord Yarstone kept to their word and stayed either alongside or not far in front. Lord Yarstone's red phaeton enjoyed a good deal of attention, a circumstance that gladdened Lilian —her sister welcomed the acclaim that she no longer wished to have. It provided a false feeling of obscurity, which Lilian, not so secretly, appreciated.

"Lady Lilian, may I have leave to call you by your given name?" Lord Harlow broke the silence. He lightly touched her gloved right hand.

Heat from his touch coiled through the core of her body, creating an unfamiliar feeling, but one she could not find disagreeable.

"I would like that, Lord Harlow…" she responded.

"John," he retorted, before she could finish. "Please call me John. Are you warm enough?" he added.

Lilian looked down at the hand he had covered with his own and realized she had hugged herself with it. How embarrassing! What must he think of her, reacting thus to his touch?

"I am warm, thank you…my…John," she answered haltingly while she studied him with curiosity. "Why are we here? I mean, why did you ask me? I am a wallflower. You could have had your pick of any young lady at the ball."

"I picked you." He lifted an eyebrow in ironic question.

Her stomach did a small flip. Lilian looked down at her hands and barely whispered.

"My lord, you flatter me. I am no longer used to such frivolity. I apologize if you deem my questions ill-mannered."

"Lilian, I have hoped for the opportunity to become reacquainted with you ever since the first time I saw you. The occasion did not arise until this week. I had begun to believe

I would not get the chance," Lord Harlow answered as he stared into her eyes.

A sigh caught in her throat and she felt her heart beat strangely fast.

"You have left me without a response," she whispered.

Lord Harlow dipped his head and pulled his horses to the right, signalling Lord Yarstone to follow. The two gentlemen turned their carriages off the main drive, slowing down as the party followed a narrower road.

He met her gaze. "I am being truthful. I realize that our first introduction was dreadful. I had hoped for better." He transferred his reins to one fist, sliding his free hand over her gloved one and squeezed gently. "Do you feel hungry?" Lord Harlow nodded towards the tree-canopied clearing ahead of them, where a small stream rippled in the dappled light. Sunshine filtered through the branches of the trees and illuminated an area of velvet-like grass. Patches of pink and white phlox covered the ground, accentuating the edges of the stream. "That looks like a perfect spot for a picnic. It is not secluded, but the traffic mostly stays on the main carriageway."

Lord Yarstone's red phaeton edged up beside them. "Would you care to picnic here?" He spoke loudly across to Lord Harlow and Lilian.

"Lady Lilian and I were discussing that possibility." Lord Harlow turned and looked at her, his blue eyes sparkling.

Lilian leaned forward to see her sister's reaction. Lydia was nodding, so she took a steadying breath.

"Yes, my lord. This would be a lovely spot." *I hope I do not regret this. Lord Harlow...John...will have to carry me to the picnic blanket.* Her heart raced a little faster at the thought of his hands holding her.

Lydia and Lord Yarstone took a blanket from each vehicle and spread them neatly beside the stream. Lord Harlow handed the reins of his curricle to his tiger and walked around to Lilian. Gently, he lifted her from the curricle. She slipped her arms around his neck. The scent of bergamot and bay leaf teased her senses, and without considering the impropriety, pulled closer. His touch, his very smell, lent her a sense of comfort and safety she had not felt since before the accident. She wanted to rest her head on his shoulder, but with belated modesty, maintained as much distance as she reasonably could. It was good fortune for her that the distance was short, or she might have succumbed.

Lord Harlow—John—tenderly placed her on the blanket next to her sister.

"Thank you...my lord." Lilian struggled with the notion of calling him by his Christian name, but in front of Lord Yarstone and her sister, she felt particularly awkward. It was too intimate, too soon. This whole adventure felt awkward, now that she thought of it. Her promise to her sister to attend one silly ball had grown into a picnic in Richmond Park with the man who had saved her life, a man whose appearance she had struggled for almost a year to recall. His fragrance had been the only thing she could remember... and now she was here with him. She shook her head.

"This will be fun!" Lydia opened the two baskets and laid out a bottle of wine, a bowl of fruits, and a small platter of cheese and meats before them. Her sister carefully poured glasses of wine, while Lilian took the plates and placed a small portion of the various meats, cheeses and bread on each.

"This is a feast!" Lilian raised her eyes to John's and took a sip. "This is very pleasant, sir. Thank you for this day." She looked over at her sister, who was sitting much closer than was proper to Lord Yarstone. That gentleman was reading Lydia a sonnet from her favourite book as they sipped wine and ignored the remainder of the repast.

"Did you hear that?" John asked soon after, setting down his emptied glass.

Lilian stilled, and John stood up, scanning the trees and along the small valley in which they sat.

"I hear something." She set her wine glass back inside the basket to keep it from spilling and listened. Persistent whimpering and weak barking sounded from behind the cluster of trees, followed by laughter.

"'Ere, I got it on the 'ead!"

"Grab its tail!"

"So? I pulled its whiskers!"

Bragging words and another bark penetrated the thick undergrowth which choked the floor of the copse beyond the trees they sat beneath.

"It sounds like an animal and some children. The animal sounds in distress."

Before they could discuss it, one boy shot through the trees, his arms holding a paw and hind leg of the poor animal, spinning it about and jeering. The other boys followed, throwing stones at a small apricot-coloured dog.

"Your turn, Ralph." The boy kicked at a smaller boy. "Do it!"

"I doesn't want to, George..." the younger boy named Ralph wailed to the larger youth. "Don't make me." Both boys wore ragged pants that barely covered their legs. Their shirts and jackets were soiled and tattered. The older boy, George, wore a flat cap, blackened with what appeared to be coal dust.

George shoved the younger boy with his elbow. "Ye missed his head, and ye owe me a penny. Take the stone and 'it 'is head," demanded the red-headed, pimply-faced youth called George. He seemed unaware he had the full attention of their party. To emphasize his point, he spun the poor animal again, holding two legs in a circle around him. The animal tried to draw its body into a ball but was too weary and merely cried in distress.

An anger such as she had never felt before welled up in Lilian. "Stop. Stop that this minute! Bring the poor animal to me." She clenched her fists beside her gown, hating that she could not get up and plant the older child a facer.

"What, me dog? What's 'e to ye?" The red-headed boy turned and at last noticed the party of adults. Dropping the puppy to the ground, still holding a rope to its neck, he folded his arms in front of him. His stance was belligerent, but Lilian noticed he maintained a safe distance from the adults. A third, dark-haired boy pulled up behind his friend, holding a fist-sized stone in his hand that he had obviously planned to pitch at the puppy's head.

"Release that animal at once!" Fury laced her voice as Lilian fought to control her temper. She detested the mistreatment of animals. She had always mended the wings of birds, taken splinters from paws, fed baby squirrels which found their way from their drey too soon. Her father had allowed her to take care of animals and, in fact, had even encouraged it. Mama, however, was not of the same mind. She did not want animals in her house, but had usually relented in the end, allowing Lilian to nurture the animals back to health.

Harlow rose to his feet and stepped in George's direction, his face mottled with anger. "I believe the lady asked you to let the animal go."

Yarstone had stopped reading and he and her sister moved to stand behind Lilian.

"Look, guvnor…this 'ere's me puppy and oi can do as oi want. 'Ye no call to tell me what to do."

Her temper flared beyond limits. Lilian would not remain quiet. She grabbed her reticule and made a great display of dumping the coins in her lap.

"Very well! I will purchase your puppy. *How much?*" she shouted. It was only a few shillings, a little pin money she kept there against emergency, but she would spend every farthing she had to save the animal.

"Lilian, you surely do not mean to bring that dog home, do you?" Lydia whispered loudly in her sister's direction.

"I do." Lilian snapped. She loved her sister, but Lydia did not see the same value in animals that she herself did. That was probably the only subject on which they truly differed. "Mama will no doubt fly up into the boughs, but she will adapt. The poor animal cannot remain with these horrid boys. They will kill it," still seething, she answered sharply, if quietly.

The red-headed boy jerked the rope hanging from the puppy's neck and nudged the dog with his dirty boot, evoking a strangled cry from the shaggy apricot-coloured mutt. At least he was no longer swinging him in a circle. The puppy whimpered loudly. Pulling on the rope, George made the animal get up on its legs and dragging it behind him, walked to her blanket. "Stupid dog. C'mere."

"I have three shillings here. I will give you all of it in exchange for the puppy." Lilian bit her lip, hoping it would be enough. She had nothing else of value with her. The poor puppy could barely stand. It appeared to be a small poodle and spaniel mix, and its matted apricot-coloured coat and its amber eyes displayed pain and fear. Crusty matter covered the inner edges of those sad eyes.

"Ain't ne'er seen 'at much money," muttered the younger boy, Ralph. "You'd pay that 'fer a dog, missus? You must be full o' juice. That be a deal of brass," he declared, thoughtfully scratching his head and looking from the puppy to the money. "'Specially since 'e ain't…"

"Stubble it, Ralph!" the pimple-faced boy screamed.

"I will add a crown." Harlow pulled a silver coin from his

pocket. "That is a considerable amount of blunt and far more than you and he are worth together. I suggest you take it and thank God for your fortune before I change my mind and have you taken up by the constable."

Lilian looked up at him appreciatively. *He cares for animals, too.*

"A fine dog, such as 'e' should bring more, if oi sell 'im." The boy smiled slyly with a fixed stare at Harlow, hoping to drive a better bargain.

Harlow took another step forward and spoke low from the back of his throat. "Do not attempt to mistake me for a flat. I could purchase a pedigree gun-dog for less than that price. You are fortunate we are prepared to pay for your mischief. However, I will not stand by while you viciously harm that puppy for entertainment. I will not allow another second of it. Take the money we have offered and leave the animal with us before I send my man for a constable. Consider carefully, for I will tell him you stole the dog from my stables a week ago."

"That's a plumper, guvnor," the boy fumed with one hand in a fist at his side. He looked at Lilian's outstretched hand and the coin Harlow held in his. "Bah! 'Tis naught but a dirty dog, after all, and 'tis a fine price. 'E's yers." George snatched the coins from Harlow and Lilian and shoved the puppy in her direction. The poor animal collapsed on her lap as the boys ran back from whence they came, the slight movement of the bushes the only sign, apart from the shivering mutt, of the entire episode. Lilian hugged the puppy close without a care for his appearance.

Harlow smiled down at her with brief amusement. "I had a fancy for a raspberry ice, but perhaps this makes for a better day."

"Lilian, he is filthy! Whatever will Mama say?"

"The same thing she said when I found the cat and her

litter of kittens. The first word will be, *no*. Then, she will list three or more reasons it is so." Lilian smiled, but inside she quaked as she wondered the same. "We can handle Mama, I am sure. I shall call my new puppy Cooper since his hair looks like copper."

"How can you tell?" Lydia asked, laughing sarcastically. "He looks the colour of mud to me." Despite her gainsaying, Lydia dropped to her knees and petted Cooper. He whined when they touched his neck, causing both girls to pull away slightly, afraid to hurt him further.

"How do you feel about the name, Cooper?" Lilian directed her question to her new puppy, who lifted his head, still trembling. His eyes were full of fear.

"I realize you are in pain at the moment," she whispered to the puppy, "but I think you will grow to like the name." Her voice was loud enough for everyone to hear, but soft enough to continue to calm her new pet. "You have a home now and we will all love you."

"He looks to be a fairly young puppy and judging from the lack of meat on his bones, half-starved," Lord Harlow observed quietly. "I have a friend who treats animals. I will ask him to call upon you, Lady Lilian."

"Thank you. I would be glad of that." She looked up and briefly squeezed his hand in appreciation. Once again, strange feelings stirred in the pit of her stomach.

Holding Cooper, Lilian lightly touched the puppy's head and tried to untie the thick hemp rope from his neck.

"I cannot get this…ah…rope free," she gasped as she struggled.

"Allow me." Lord Yarstone reached down to the blanket beside him and picked up the paring knife he had used on the fruit. "This should work." He carefully sawed at the rope until the dirty length of hemp broke.

The rope had rubbed the puppy's neck raw, leaving it

hairless, red and weeping with blood. Lilian took an embroidered handkerchief from her reticule and dabbed it into her wine glass. She comforted Cooper.

"Poor little one, this may sting, but it will help, I promise." Gently, she wiped some white wine over the area. Cooper stood still and gave her hand a small lick when she had finished.

"This should make him more comfortable, Lady Lilian." Lord Harlow had stepped to his vehicle and pulled a plaid blanket from the box beneath his seat.

"Thank you, sir." Lilian accepted the blanket and Lord Harlow squatted down and helped her wrap the blanket around the trembling, overwhelmed animal. Cooper's nose nuzzled her chest, and he edged himself in as close to a cuddle with Lilian as he could manage.

"I am done for!" Lord Harlow laughed jokingly. "I gave my coin and have created new competition for your attentions."

"Nonsense," she answered good-naturedly, then glancing at her sister. "We should return home and introduce Cooper to Mama as soon as possible. You are right, Lydia. She will not be happy."

"The food is almost gone, but I will bet that the little fellow would love to have some meat, bread and cheese." Lord Yarstone brought his basket close, holding out a leftover half loaf of bread. Cooper sniffed and strained to reach it.

"Good man, Yarstone. Perhaps we should give him some bread and make sure he fills his belly. I would go easy on the cheeses and meat. The spicier ones could make him sick. I have a bottle of water here." Lord Harlow offered the water in a small bowl. After swallowing the small loaf almost whole, the puppy thirstily lapped the water.

"He is starving!" Lilian burst out. "We should get him

home immediately. Lydia, I will need your help to get him bathed and his hair trimmed. I think we should do it together. He trusts us," she added, with great satisfaction.

She hugged Cooper closer to her heart and smiled. This had been a good day, so far. She had done a good deed, not allowing her infirmity to stop her, and she had a new friend. She could not regret that. Now all she needed was good fortune, she thought brightly.

CHAPTER 6

"A *puppy?*" Lady Avalon fairly choked on the words but quickly calmed herself. "You went for a drive in the park. Whatever do you mean, you brought back a dog, Lilian?" Her mother punctuated her name slowly. "No, my dear, I am afraid we cannot keep him. You know that there are several reasons why we cannot have a dog."

This must be the list Lilian had spoken of. Harlow swallowed the urge to laugh; beside him, Lilian sighed.

Lady Avalon held out her fingers one by one, quickly ticking off each reason as she stared at Cooper cowering in Lilian's arms.

"First of all, Cook has enough to do without having to prepare meals for a puppy. In addition, a puppy needs constant maintenance and care. He will bring those parasites —fleas, I believe they are called—into the house. I cannot tolerate it," she added for emphasis. "And you know your father will not appreciate another stray animal being brought into the house. The birds and the cats were one thing…a puppy is much more demanding of attention. That is wholly different."

The door opened and Lord Avalon walked into the room. "Did someone mention me? Chambers told me you girls had returned. I was coming out of my office just now and I noticed a bit of a to-do in the hall. Since you ladies are given to frequenting the parlour, I presumed there might be some interesting goings-on in here...more engaging than working on my accounts, at any rate!" Lilian's father chuckled as he moved further into the packed room. The parlour already contained his family, one puppy, Lord Yarstone and Harlow himself.

This feels awkward, he thought, *but sometimes life can be more humorous than fiction.* There had not been a suitable moment to say goodbye. Harlow glanced at Lilian, who was sitting in her chair, holding the animal and giving her mother her full attention, yet at the same time discreetly adjusting the puppy so that her mother could see Cooper's face. He recognized her simple strategy and admired her guileful approach.

"My dear, I did, but it was in explanation of why we cannot keep this puppy." Lady Avalon answered calmly, pointing to Cooper. Her tone contrasted sharply with the diatribe she had just given. She was clearly nonplussed with the situation.

"Yes...yes, I have just noticed the poor creature." He turned to Lilian. "I suppose you have given him a name?" he questioned lightly. "You always do." Lord Avalon raised a bushy black and grey eyebrow and tried to look irritated. He was failing miserably, in Harlow's opinion. This sympathy with animals was a side to Lilian that he had not expected. It reminded him of his own childhood. He had spent every spare minute with his father's dogs or their horses, including helping the grooms to tend the injured ones.

"Cooper," Lilian proffered. She put her pet down and

watched the sorry animal walk to her mother's feet and look up at the woman.

The older man chuckled. "The dog is a sharp one, so he is. How did you come by him, daughter?"

Lilian quickly related Cooper's sad tale to her father, who walked over and accepted the puppy, dirt and all. Lord Avalon scratched him behind the ear for a moment and then held the puppy up in front of him.

"I can see you are a mighty personable little fellow under all this mud and muck." He looked at his daughter, who had not taken her eyes from the two of them. "Lilian, we must..." He hesitated a moment, as if searching for the right word. "Cooper needs a bath, a comfortable bed and a good meal," he finished at last. "You may ask Clara to request some scraps for his dinner from Cook. Allow your mother and I to discuss this and we will speak more on it tonight." Her father chucked the puppy playfully under his chin and smiled encouragingly in his daughter's direction before putting the puppy down and supplying a more austere look to the rest in the room. Harlow noticed the change only because he was standing near Lilian and realized Lord Avalon only smiled while his back was to his Countess. The Earl and his wife left the room, ostensibly to discuss the animal, Harlow presumed. Lord Yarstone, the sisters, Cooper and Harlow himself were left in the parlour.

Lydia smiled at her sister and patted Cooper on the head. "I think Father will convince her. I have no notion what magic you possess with Father, Lilian, but he can never deny you anything," Lydia said candidly, and laughed.

"We each have our strengths, dear sister. Mama can refuse you naught, as well. That is why we have always complemented each other," Lilian added quietly.

"I think you are right. We cannot expect this always to be the case, but it would seem the fates do lean in that direction.

Father supports my sister's mischief and Mama finds less fault with mine," Lydia added, gurgling with laughter. Lilian smiled too, yet it seemed somewhat forced.

"It is time I took my leave," Harlow remarked quietly.

"Thank you for a most pleasant excursion, sir." Lilian looked up at him. She was once again holding Cooper.

"Then I shall bid you farewell." Harlow lifted Lilian's gloved hand and gave it a light kiss. "I enjoyed the outing, Lady Lilian, and look forward to the next. If you will give me leave, I should very much like to call on you again."

"I should be pleased to welcome you, Lord Harlow. Thank you for your many kindnesses," Lilian responded, a red blush creeping up her face as she tucked her new dog closer with her other arm.

He patted Cooper. "Be a good boy, now, sir. I will dispatch a good friend of mine, a Mr. Whitten, to help with your injuries," he added.

"Thank you, John," Lilian mouthed quietly.

"I am afraid I must also take my leave, Lady Lydia," Lord Yarstone added. He kissed Lydia's outstretched hand and gave a quick bow. "I too look forward to seeing you again."

"I reciprocate your sentiments, sir," Lady Lydia responded, her face glowing with evident contentment.

Chambers waited at the front door, holding their hats and gloves. Harlow and Lord Yarstone accepted their items and walked down the steps together.

"That was awkward," Harlow uttered when the door closed behind them. "I did not get the feeling Chambers disliked us, earlier. However, of a certainty, I detected a certain level of displeasure in his actions just now."

"I believe he dislikes the puppy," Yarstone offered, chuckling. "But I think the dog will stay. Odd, is it not, that he would display such an aversion though?"

"I believe you could be right, my friend. Did you collect

how Lady Avalon's argument turned to dust the minute Lord Avalon came into the room?" He was certain Lord Avalon would accept the puppy. "I will bet that the puppy is being bathed as we speak."

"I never bet against a certainty," Yarstone added, laughing. "There seemed to be some urgency, at least on Lady Avalon's part."

Chuckling amicably, both men turned to their carriages.

"I cannot imagine the last time the little critter had more than a rain shower. It will want for naught, now. Lady Lilian will dote on him," reflected Harlow.

"Wait." Lord Yarstone came up from behind him. "I need to say something."

Yarstone touched him on the shoulder as Harlow was about to mount into his curricle.

"I apologize, Harlow, for my unforgivable jealousy earlier today."

Harlow bit back a smile. "Give it no further thought, my friend. I understood. Lady Lydia is a beautiful lady. It is obvious you are making a claim for her. I think she may feel the same way," he added. "For myself, I prefer…"

"Lady Lilian," Yarstone supplied, smiling.

"Yes. I like her, but I need to give serious thought to anything further. I do not know if I am ready for marriage as much as my mother would like me to be." He winced, thinking about his mother. She would undoubtedly hear of his courtship of Lady Lilian and have expectations and questions—lots of questions.

"May I offer a word of advice, Harlow?"

"Yes, I suppose I could accept that. It does not mean I will agree." His lips twitched.

"I had a similar situation with my family. My own mother was making me uncomfortable by parading eligible misses under my nose and insisting I squire her to parties, where she paraded me to all her bosom-bows. It came to the point where I could not bear to go home, so I decided to broach the subject. I had naught to lose." Yarstone paused a moment. "I spoke with Mother and explained how her faradiddles and tricks and stratagems, however well-meant, made me feel. I told her I had no desire to let the title leave the family but would make my own decisions at my own pace."

"And how did that go with your mother?" Harlow was very interested. He all but avoided his mother because of her machinations. Perhaps a straightforward approach would be for the best. It made sense. *As Yarstone said, what have I to lose?*

"She apologized and said she would try. That is all I can ask of her, in truth." Yarstone reached his hand out to Harlow, who shook it.

"Thank you, Yarstone. I have not thought to be clear with Mother. Perhaps it is time." *It would also give me time to reflect,* he added, finishing his thought.

"One more thing, Harlow." Yarstone looked serious.

"Yes?"

"I noticed a woman watching us in the park today, from a distance. I made no comment on it to Lady Lydia, and as far as I am aware, she took no note of the occurrence."

"You did? Where? Did you recognize this woman?" Harlow's breath caught in his throat, hoping he had not twice put the lady he considered so beautiful in danger.

"I believe it was the widow, Lady Poinz. I noticed her at the ball the other night, dressed in red satin. Somewhat hard to miss, that one." He smiled wryly.

"Yes. Lady Catherine Poinz is hard to ignore." *Extremely so,* he thought. *Perhaps that bears more discussion.*

"She was walking with a gentleman I did not recognize. I could not see him clearly; the large plumes on her hat hid his face," Yarstone stated. "They were walking along the path beside a stream. I was behind you and noticed her staring in your direction, looking anything but appreciative in her demeaner, if you get my meaning. They stopped and watched when you turned off the pathway to the small picnic site. I suppose I have become somewhat protective of the DeLacey ladies," he admitted slowly.

"I did not notice Lady Poinz today, and I thank you for this information. She is an old acquaintance. I met with her briefly at the party." He laughed it off, hoping to convince Yarstone of his sincerity. "I am afraid the lady makes more of our acquaintance than I ever have. Perhaps it startled her to see me in the park." This was becoming difficult. He would speak with Catherine as soon as he could and try to determine why she was staring at him in such a fashion. "Yarstone..."

"I should have no objections should we be on first name terms," Yarstone put in, "if that is acceptable to you. I am thinking we are like to meet a good deal in the future." He stretched out his hand. "Richard." As an afterthought, he added, "I trust you do not plan to toy with Lady Lilian's affections...?"

Harlow cut him off. "I assure you, I do not intend to do that. I understand your concerns and I assure you there is naught between the widow Poinz and myself. Nevertheless, I thank you for this information, Richard." He took the Viscount's hand. "Most of my friends call me Harlow and that suits my inclinations." Harlow bent his head in quick acknowledgement before they separated. He handed the reins to his tiger and sat back for the drive to his club. He needed to think.

His tiger pulled the horses to a stop in front of White's. "Pick me up in two hours, Simmons."

"Yes, my lord." The tiger touched his hat. "I'll be 'ere."

"Get yourself something to eat while you are about it, Simmons," he said, placing a crown in his driver's hand.

"Thank ye, m'lord." The driver gave a cheerful grin and tucked the coin in his pocket.

"One more thing." Harlow looked up at the driver. "Did you see a…I hesitate to call her a lady…a rather striking woman in the park when we turned off the main pathway earlier?

"Hard t'miss 'er, m'lord. She 'ad on a yeller and black striped dress and black plumes to the moon." The wiry little man cackled. "Ay, Mr. Moore and the lady was walking near the brook when we turned."

"Mr. Moore? The man who owns the Golden Goose Public House?" This piece of news intrigued Harlow.

"'Oi believe so, m'lord. I knows nuthin 'bout his own'ns, but it were him right enough," Simmons responded with certainty.

How curious. Harlow was not sure if he had said this out loud or not.

"Thank you, Simmons."

Harlow handed over his hat and gloves upon entering White's and inquired after his friend. Max sat exactly where the major-domo had told him he would be, tucked into a heavy, red leather chair by the fireplace, sipping an amber-coloured liquor, which Harlow surmised to be his favourite brandy. He was seated at a heavy table with matching chairs in a circle.

He took the seat next to Max, appreciating the low-burning embers. They took the chill from the room but did not overheat it. Harlow accepted a glass of his favourite whisky and leaned back, his mood reflective. He favoured this chair, mostly because of the room it gave him to stretch his legs and rest. If he leaned back just enough, it could touch a wall behind him and he could stretch out his legs a little more. Doing so, he soon relaxed. His legs instantly felt better.

"How are Meg and baby Nathan doing?" he queried. "I am

surprised you would come to Town and leave them, so soon after Nathan's birth.".

"They are both doing splendidly. Shep stands guard over the baby. It took a week to become accustomed to seeing him extend that protective nature of his to the baby. Nathan is almost the same size as he is." Max laughed. "But he is very loyal. I take a distant third place behind the two of them. Before Nathan was born, I had to chase my socks around. Now, I am barely noticed."

"Your mother must have been delighted," Harlow said, a wry smile lifting the corner of his mouth. "Please do not encourage her to contact my mother. Mother has been at her old tricks again, scouring the debutantes for the lady she deems to be the one for me. It has become so bad, I shall be forced to speak with her about it."

"You do that, my friend. Let me know your secret if it works—or I will send the notice of your sad demise to the papers." A sardonic smile flickered on Max's lips as he sipped his drink.

"Highly amusing, Max. Although you are right. It will not be easy." Harlow considered his friend's words. "Max," he said in a low voice after a pause, "We have a few matters to discuss."

"I agree," Max said, avidly. "Have you seen the latest bet in the book?" He lightly hit the palm of his hand on the table to emphasize his enthusiasm.

The betting book at White's contained some of the latest gossip, with outrageous bets making up some *on-dits* even more noteworthy. Harlow never wished to be one of those designated unfortunates who had their names penned beside a bet.

He leaned further into his chair, allowing a smile to crease his face. This had to be one of Max's jokes. He would not take the bait.

"Well, now. I am all ears. What does it say?"

"One hundred pounds on you becoming a tenant for life with one Lady Lilian DeLacey."

All of a sudden, the chair Harlow had been leaning back in crashed to the floor.

CHAPTER 7

A day later

"Come on, Cooper. Wake up, little fellow." Lilian reached into the large straw basket that Clara had made into a bed and lifted the drowsy puppy, cradling him in her arms. Father had told her he planned to ask a man Lord Harlow had recommended to check Cooper's health before he had access to the whole house. Mama had relented when she and Father had discussed the dog. Lilian suspected her father had taken a liking to the little fellow.

A knock on the door sounded, and Mama popped her head inside the room. "Lilian, I asked the housekeeper to clean out the linen closet. She has found two blankets which have not been used in some time. I thought you might find them useful for Cooper." Her mother did not wait for an invitation to hold the puppy and held out her hands.

"Oh, what a sweet little rascal," Lady Avalon said, tickling his belly lightly with her fingernails.

Who was this woman pretending to be her mother? "Mama, you are sure you do not mind Cooper being here, are you not?" Over the years, her mother had relented to Lilian's various acquisitions. Not once, however, had she come to play with the pet in question. She had always maintained a reserved distance from the offending animal or bird. This, Lilian mused, was quite extraordinary. She fought the impulse to ring for Clara, to send for the doctor, and instead relished the pure joy her mother was displaying with the newest family member. Cooper lay in a relaxed pose, allowing her to scratch his belly—obviously enjoying himself, too.

Unexpectedly, Mama whipped her hand into her pocket and withdrew a small blue ball, to which she had tied a string of yarn. Cooper's eyes lit up at the sight of it, and he immediately wriggled to be set down.

Lilian watched in utter surprise as her mother repeatedly threw the ball and pulled it back, teasing Cooper into chasing it. The little dog became thrilled and immediately threw himself into the activity, forgetting the ailments they had been nursing only a day before.

"Fetch it, Cooper!" Her mother threw the ball and pulled it back, provoking Cooper to bite and paw at the ball, determined to claim it. Lilian laughed with full-throated glee when he almost caught it, an image which hearkened back to childhood, teasing her memory.

"Mama, have you ever had a dog of your own?" Lilian asked, not sure where the question came from. In fact, she had not even thought about the question before asking. It just popped out of her mouth.

Her mother put the ball away and scooped up the shaggy apricot-coloured puppy, kissed his nose and turned to her daughter.

"Mama, what is wrong?" Lilian grew concerned. Her mother's eyes filled with tears. "I once had a dog of my own. Her name was Rascal. You were very small."

"I remember!" That was the memory which had fought for a footing in her mind.

"She was a small, terrier-type breed; white with brown spots on her, and we had had her for several years. You may not remember her, but Rascal loved to follow you around as you toddled. Lydia, I recall, was not as enamoured of the dog, but you loved touching her and would coo her name. Rascal was protective of you both." Her mother dabbed at the corners of her eyes.

"Your father and I left for London for a week. When we returned, the servants had lost Rascal. No one had sent word to us, or we surely would have returned sooner. Everyone in the household searched, afraid they would lose their jobs because they knew how much I loved her."

She drew a deep breath and paused for a moment. "We finally found her, but when we got to Rascal, she was barely alive. The poor thing had become locked in the basement of the chapel. It seemed she had fallen in through a broken window and nearly starved." Her mother sat up and dabbed her eyes again. "I have not spoken to anyone, save your father, about Rascal until just this moment. I thought the pain would never stop and the guilt at not being there felt insurmountable." Lady Avalon placed her hand over her pocket and hugged it closer to her. "Rascal was a birthday present from my papa," she whispered. "He gave her to me at my own coming out. To lose her felt as though I had lost a part of myself."

"I am so sorry, Mama. I did not understand. I might have behaved differently had I known."

"Nonsense! Your father made me come to terms with this,

and I want to apologize for my prejudice on the subject. I hope you can forgive me." She leaned down and kissed Cooper on the top of his head. "I love the name, dearest." Putting Cooper down on the bed between them, she hugged Lilian. "You challenge me in so many ways. I want so much for both you and Lydia, yet it is no more than every mother wants for her daughters." Her mother once more wiped her eyes, and a small smile shaped her lips, although it was accompanied by a deep intake of breath. "Lord Harlow has sent word that he has asked a friend of his, a Mr. Mark Whitten, to come and examine Cooper for you. According to your father, he should arrive sometime today."

Lilian did not quite know what to say. She was both shocked and delighted by this new side to her mother. Cooper, it seemed, was also quite taken with Mama.

Affording full credit to Lord Harlow, Mama explained that since the puppy was not having any problems beyond near-starvation and rope burns, Mr. Whitten felt he could time his visit when he came to Town to attend the Veterinary College.

"It seems he is a young farrier," Mama explained, "and has ambitions of becoming a horse doctor. He lives in the county of Essex, where he assists the farmers with all their stock, dogs included."

Timing was a funny thing, Lilian thought to herself, reflecting on the timing of their discovery of Cooper before more damage had been done. Father had asked her how much she had paid for the dog. She had told him truthfully; to her surprise, his demeanour had not changed. He had merely commented that the boys would most likely have better use for the money than the poor, starving puppy. Her father never showed his temper, but that was his way. He understood her. In contrast, she never felt she knew Mama, although this new facet of her personality made her very happy. Perhaps having a puppy was something they could all enjoy.

The bed shifted as Mama stood up, absently brushing wrinkles free from her skirt.

"Before I leave, I have something to give you." She fished into her pocket and withdrew a small, braided collar of red leather. "This was Rascal's. I would like it very much if you would let Cooper wear it." A small silver tag hung from a metal loop near the buckle, inscribed with the words, *Cooper. Much loved.* "Father secured the inscription for me. It has room to expand as he grows, as long as it is not too much." She added, pointing out a small amount of extra leather beyond the buckle.

It was Lilian's turn to wipe away her tears. "Thank you, Mama. That is the sweetest gift you have ever given to me. I will treasure it always, and I think Cooper will be proud to wear it. I should probably attach it to his basket until his neck heals." She leaned over and secured the collar to Cooper's basket and then lovingly smoothed his head.

Her mother smiled warmly, squeezing her daughter's shoulder with palpable affection.

"Now then, I should see Cook about Cooper's meals. It is my belief that dogs do well with a small amount of vegetables in their meals, although not onions or turnips," her mother said thoughtfully. "They are never good, so I must instruct Cook to prepare the proper amount of meat and vegetables for him. Perhaps a small portion of rusks." She patted Cooper once more and left the room.

Lilian leaned back against her pillows in a slight state of shock. Her mother was suddenly more jovial and easier to speak with—all because of one small apricot-coloured dog. Cooper stepped out of the basket and walked up to her, nudging her chin with the tip of his nose.

"Cooper, look what Mama has brought for you. 'Tis a

proper collar. Once your neck is better, I will let you wear it and you will look very suitable!" Scooping up the little dog, she cuddled him, and then rang for Clara. She wanted to get dressed and begin her day. It was pretty outside, and she suddenly had the desire to toss a ball with her new puppy.

Five minutes later, her maid came into the room. "M'lady, 'tis time for Cooper to step outside afore he breaks his fast." The older woman cackled softly. "I have not seen your mother this happy fer years, not since her Rascal passed away."

Lilian was grateful that Mama had reminded her of Rascal; otherwise, she would not have understood Clara's remark. Usually she would ignore such ramblings by her old nurse and not ask questions, but she understood Mama now, and also recalled Rascal. She felt honoured by her mother's gesture.

"M'lady, yer parents asked me to tell you they 'ave decided to leave for Tintagel on the morrow. M'bones cannot wait for the fresh air of the sea again. I will pack your trunks tonight.

Fifteen minutes later saw Lilian being transported to the first floor with Cooper following behind.

"Winston, thank you." Lilian acknowledged the young footman who always helped her move about the town house. She wheeled herself to the table, where a plate with various offerings from the sideboard was ready for her to break her fast.

Musing over the day in front of her, she realized she would miss London—or at least two things about London. One of those was Lord Harlow. She felt a quickening in her stomach at the thought of him, similar to the jolts she felt when he was near her. Lord Harlow had not been to visit for two days, now. *Surely, I have not developed a fondness for him... have I?* A gurgle of laughter escaped her throat. *I miss him.* He had been in her mind for the past year, a faceless man who had saved her, calming her at the very time she needed a calm touch. His warm, baritone voice and haunting scent had soothed her senses, somehow connecting with her very soul.

As much as she missed her home in Tintagel, where the bedroom was on the second floor instead of here, on the third floor of a townhouse. And her horse was stabled there, no doubt eating his head off in his stall. However, she would miss spending time with...John. She tried to think of him by his given name instead of Lord Harlow, as he had asked.

Gently spearing a piece of the orange from her plate, she ate, still lost in her thoughts. Aside from her sister, Danby was her best friend. Lilian often spent hours with him in the stable, using a chair placed near his stall for her use. On bright days, she took a book to read. His velvety brown nose often cajoled her into smiling, no matter her mood. *I wonder how Danby will get on with Cooper. Stop worrying. He will love the little rapscallion.*

The sound of light boot-steps sounded behind her and broke her contemplation. Her mother partly opened the door to the room.

"Lilian, my dear, Mr. Whitten has arrived."

Lilian patted her knees. "Cooper, up!" The little dog hopped up onto her lap, and they rolled along into the hall together.

"Perhaps we should go into the parlour. The room is bright, and there is plenty of space. I will have some tea brought." Without waiting for a reply, her mother left again.

Lilian and Cooper wheeled into the parlour, followed by Mr. Whitten.

"I understand you have named the puppy?" He squatted down and gently patted Cooper's head, while examining the raw places on his neck. "That is a fine name, Cooper. It fits him." He paused and looked up. "I also understand he could have been hurt badly had you not intervened on his behalf. What good fortune you have had, little chap," Mr. Whitten added with a serious look on his face.

Lilian felt a twinge of pride at his words.

Whitten continued his examination, scrutinizing Cooper's teeth, his paws, his belly and his ears.

"Soft belly. No drainage from his eyes or nose. Very good," he continued aloud, but almost to himself. Whitten felt along the dog's spine and checked the area under his tail. "No sign of worms or other parasites." He pulled out his stethoscope and listened to Cooper's heart. "Strong. No abnormal sounds." Whitten then gently rolled Cooper onto his back and looked at his paws.

Amazed, Lilian looked on while her small puppy complied without complaint.

"I was told that he was being swung around by his legs. A disgraceful way to treat an animal, in my opinion. He is fortunate, as I do not feel any tender spots. His joints feel as they should." Whitten patted Cooper on the head, signalling the end of the examination. "I have a tincture that I will leave for his neck area. Twice a day, take a cloth, wet it in diluted vinegar and gently dab that on the open areas. He may not like it, but it should help the sores to heal." He pulled a small bottle from his bag and placed it in her hand. "This tincture of myrrh and aloes should help. Sprinkle it lightly and wait a few minutes. This ointment applied fifteen minutes after the tincture should help clear things up. Only apply a thin coat. The cool air will help with healing. In a few days, I think he will be as good as new and his coat will grow back."

"Thank you, Mr. Whitten. Do you know his age?" Lilian was delighted to get such a good report.

"If I were to hazard a guess, I estimate he is five or six months old. Remarkably, he seems not to have gained worms or any other pestilence. Many puppies succumb to them early. This little puppy is remarkably healthy." He turned to Cooper. "Take good care of your mistress, Cooper, I believe she will take care of you." As he spoke, Whitten packed his bag.

Lady Avalon, who had quietly returned to the room while the examination was going on, rose and walked over to Lilian's chair.

"Mr. Whitten, will you take a cup of tea and some biscuits? A maid is bringing some light refreshments." At that moment, the maid walked in with the tea tray and placed it on the table near them.

"Thank you, my lady, but I feel I should be on my way. I have a horse I must attend near Smithfield Market." He bowed politely. "Good day to you."

"Of course." Lady Avalon nodded. "Good day. Before you leave, my husband asked that you wait on him in his study. I believe he wishes to thank you personally."

"I will do that." He turned to Lilian. "It has been a pleasure to meet you, my lady. Lord Harlow spoke at length about the young woman who took on a small gang of curs to rescue a small puppy," he said cheerily. "I could see he was greatly impressed."

"Thank you, sir. You are very kind. I am sure I did no more than many in my place would have done." Lilian's face reddened slightly at the compliment and the reminder of John Andrews.

"Of course. All the same, it was a good thing for the animal that you intervened when you did." Whitten smiled politely, picked up his bag, and left the room.

"Mama, I will send a note to Lord Harlow, thanking him for his kindness." Without waiting for a reply, Lilian wheeled her chair to the tall secretaire against the wall, opened the desk and extracted paper.

"That would be the proper thing to do," her mother

rejoined in a distracted tone. Lilian glanced over her shoulder at her mother, who was sitting on the couch, holding Cooper. The puppy was giving her licks on the chin.

"Astonishing," she muttered to herself as she wrote a note to John.

CHAPTER 8

Harlow wondered if Max was bamboozling him about his getting leg-shackled to Lady Lilian. Once he had picked himself up, apologized for breaking the chair and blotted the drink from his pantaloons with his handkerchief, he walked over to the Betting Book and checked for himself.

"Fustian nonsense!" he declared. Sure enough, someone had written 'per L.C.P to one M.M.' He knew other gentlemen with the initials M.B, but none that would have plastered this about Town. The 'per L.C.P' threw him. "This has to be some sort of lark. Who would post such as thing?"

"It appears that M.M. put forward the wager. Do you know him?" Max asked, sauntering up to join him. "More to the point, perchance you should inform your old friend about Lady Lilian," he prodded jokingly. "By Jove! Is that the young lady who was thrown from her horse last year?"

"The same," growled Harlow. He enjoyed Lady Lilian's company, and had planned to call on her today, so why did he feel as though his under-carriage had been displayed for all the world? It did not affect just him, either. It called attention to Lady Lilian, a lady who sought privacy. His attention had cast her into public notice. He instantly regretted his initial, selfish reflections on how this affected him. "I need to find this M.M. and have him erase that bet." It was not something he could do on his own. Once a bet was cast, it stayed unless it was cancelled by the one who had it entered on the pages. At least, he hoped it could be expunged.

"You will catch cold at this, my friend. What do you know? I go out of Town for a few days, and when I come back, what do I find? You, all but caught in parson's mousetrap! Is this decision not something you consider worthy of sharing with your friends?" Max asked nonchalantly, examining his cuticles.

"I will not have the lady's name bandied about in public, Max!" Harlow hissed. He glanced about to make sure they could not be overheard and lowered his voice. "She is Lord Avalon's daughter, if you must have it, and no, I am not about to be engaged."

"Do you like her?" Max persisted, a smile teasing the corners of his lips.

Max liked to taunt him, but he should understand this more than most. He knew from experience that Harlow still had nightmares. How often had they been forced to share close quarters while undertaking a commission together?

"You know I cannot marry."

"That is not what I asked," Max replied calmly. "Perhaps the right woman would make a difference in that aspect of your life…but do go on."

"I am aware of what you asked, and yes, I enjoy her company. I suppose I would not be averse to marrying her, if I were in the market to marry," Harlow admitted. "Conjecture is worthless, however, for I am not," he added emphatically.

"And this is because of the nightmares? Perhaps if you

were to talk about what haunts you, it could help," Max asserted in a sober tone.

"Nothing can help me, Max." The two men returned to their table.

"I am serious, nonetheless. Perhaps marriage would be good for you; ease the strain of whatever burdens dog you, if you were to find the right lady. Someone who would listen to your thoughts and concerns."

Harlow opened his mouth to respond but stopped. He knew many others who complained of the nightmares after the wars with France. Perhaps Max could be right... No! Whatever was he thinking? Lilian had her own nightmare. He would not add to her troubles. He would find whoever was responsible for this outrage and have them cancel the entry. In the meantime, he hoped people would ignore it.

"I know what you are thinking." Max grinned and held up his hand, signalling the waiter to bring them another round of drinks. "No one will miss that. And the page is only half-filled. They will see it for a long time."

A waiter returned and quietly refreshed their drinks.

"I know." Harlow caught the defeated tone in his own voice and decided he would not allow himself to fall in a dudgeon over this. He also realized, with alarming clarity, that he could not just abandon Lady Lilian, not given the attention he had already paid her. That would be wrong. "You say you have known people to recover from these nightmares?" He wanted to hear about that.

"I have." Max pushed the refreshed drink in Harlow's direction. "I think, however, it would be better to discuss that somewhere less...public. Since you cracked the legs of that chair, our fellow members, who are studiously avoiding looking this way, are nevertheless cocking their ears avidly in our direction."

"Let me tell you what I know," Harlow offered. He bent

his head down and talked in a low voice. "First, I want to tell you about the carriage that almost ran me over, two days ago, on its way to the Golden Goose Public House."

"On Duke Street?" Max sat upright. "Michael 'Bowie' Moore owns it. Not an unfamiliar name, I am finding, to the smuggling world."

"I think that was its destination. The horses careened around the corner, and as I passed, I spotted the same horses, with their heads tossing back and forth in irritation, frothing from the pace of it all. They were just visible at the rear of the alehouse."

"Bowie was a name given to me by a contact in London, last week. I think it bears further investigation. He may have the name, but they know him as a reputable businessman in London, at least on one side of the aisle. We need to be sure before we connect him to anything. Maybe there are others associated with him. I will get someone to look into that."

"The whole episode was odd. I was on my way to meet..." he paused, realizing what he was about to say. "...Lady Lilian," he finished slowly. He waited for the ribald response. It did not come.

"This could be a sign, my friend," Max said mildly, slapping him on the back.

"You cannot let the hound lie sleeping, can you?" Harlow countered with good-humoured relief.

"No, I fear not. I cannot say I am sorry for it, though." Max coughed into his fist, signalling they were no longer alone. A man with shoulder-length hair and an ill-fitting blackcoat, tattered at the sleeves had appeared from the side of the building and seemed to be watching them.

"Do you care to indulge me in a round at Gentleman Jackson's? I feel the need for some exercise before we return to Tintagel." Harlow stood up and grabbed his cane. He did not always carry it with him, unless he was doing the pretty in Town, as Max would term it. Half the time he spent trying to remember where he had left it. His mother had given him the wooden cane with a dog on the handle. Since it reminded him of his childhood pet, he hoped he could keep it. The sight of the dog brought forth another detail he needed to tell Max. "There is one other thing that I found odd that same day. Viscount Yarstone spotted Lady Catherine Poinz watching us picnic in Richmond Park the other day."

"You took a picnic in Richmond Park?" Max widened his eyes. "Mayhap I need to know more about Lady Lilian. To return to your point, though: that is odd. I came across the widow at the milliner's yesterday. I was picking up a new hat, and she was walking out of the milliner's next door with a footman behind her carrying several boxes. She stopped and asked if I was planning to be in London very long. Most odd."

"What did you say to her?" Harlow asked.

"You know me better than that. I smiled and complimented her atrocious purple and black plumed hat, tipped my own hat and went inside. I heard the busy-body clear her throat in a disapproving way—*you know*—as she continued past me."

"'Tis odd that she keeps popping up," Harlow said absently. "L.C.P…Lady Catherine Poinz!"

"Curious. She saw you in the park with Lady Lilian, you said?" Max looked thoughtful. "How could she do that? Who would post a bet using her initials? I know, you will say, M.M.—but White's is the stiffest of all the gentlemen's clubs."

"It makes sense, nevertheless. This bears watching. I will find out who M.M. is. Perhaps, all I have to do is discover who is having a dalliance with Lady Poinz."

"Maybe." Max rubbed his chin. "We will not solve this now. What say you we head to Gentleman Jackson's? I too feel the need for exercise now."

"Agreed."

"My carriage is around the corner. Simmons can set us down and pick us up in two hours," Harlow offered.

"That sounds like a good idea. The weather is warm, after all. I doubt we will want to be seen on the toddle after the match." Max sniggered.

"True enough." The two men walked outside and met Simmons, who stood ready at the coach. "Simmons, take us to Gentleman Jackson's Boxing Saloon," Harlow directed. He needed the release of strenuous exercise. A bout of fisticuffs was a good idea. He just hoped he did not come home with bruises. They tried to avoid faces when they sparred, but sometimes the best-laid schemes could still go awry. "Devilish good idea, Max. Planting you a facer is just what I need!" Harlow eased himself into the squabs of the seat and stared at the passing street.

"You have more chance of slipping one past Jackson's guard. I shall take great delight in drawing your cork," Max said coolly. On the whole, they were evenly matched. Max was broader in the shoulders and it gave him greater reach. At least that is how Harlow excused any failure to his dark-haired friend.

"You think to bait me into taking some advantage, so that when I beat you," Harlow emphasized the last word, "you can accuse me of winning by advantage. I am wise to your tricks!"

They fell into a familiar silence as the carriage travelled through the streets to Bond Street. As it slowed down, from the corner of his eye Harlow caught sight of a large navy plume gently waving. Rapidly, he pulled back his head and, taking his cane, indicated for Simmons to keep driving.

"Max, she is here."

"Who are you talking about?" Max asked, sounding alarmed.

"I do not think she was looking in our direction when we drove by, but it was Lady Poinz. I recognized her. She was staring at the door to the boxing academy," he said flatly, "just as she was watching at the park. She is here again. It seems far too much of a coincidence to me."

"But we are not in there yet. Are you sure she is watching you?" Max spoke low, although there was no one but Simmons to hear.

"Not with any certainty. However, do you not think it is a bit strange? London seems too large a place to run into the same person so often—three times in almost as many days." Harlow reduced his own voice to a loud whisper. "We are approaching the saloon again. I shall signal for Simmons to stop this time." He rapped the cane on the roof of the coach. "We have a code," he said, chuckling at Max, who had confusion etched all over his face.

The carriage came to a stop and the two men hopped out. The woman in question stood staring at the door to the boxing academy.

"Good morning, Lady Poinz," Harlow and Max said almost together. Both tipped their hats.

"Good morning!" Her tone was all sugary. "What are you two gentlemen doing at the saloon? Do you plan to work up a good sweat?" She casually licked her bottom lip as she gazed in Harlow's direction.

If he had ever found anything remotely fascinating about the woman, it was a thing of the past. Her unsubtle coquetry filled his stomach with disgust, a feeling he was not used to experiencing when with a female—but this woman was no lady.

"Such an odd place to run into you, Lady Poinz," Harlow retorted lightly. "We do not see too many women outside Gentleman Jackson's Saloon."

"That is a shame, because I think this is a most wonderful

part of London. Men go in, and men come out…looking as though they need a little extra attention," she added, a sardonic gleam in her eyes. Seductively, she stepped closer and ran her gloved finger down the front of Harlow's shirt, stopping at the fall of his breeches. He grabbed her hand.

"Lady Poinz…" Harlow's tone was menacing. "…never touch my body unless you are invited to do so. I do not know what game it is you are playing, but I want nothing to do with it."

"So you say, dearest, but I fear you may be mistaken." She looked him up and down, her gaze lingering on his lower half.

"We have business to attend, Lady Poinz. Good day to you." Harlow tugged on his hat, refusing to give her any more courtesy, and walked into the building. What was her game?

Max followed Harlow inside. "She seems to be looking for someone. Give me a minute. Harlow gave his hat and cane to a footman who was waiting to assist them and then walked to the side of the nearest window to look out. She continued to stare at the door of the academy until a weathered black carriage pulled up. A short man with a moustache opened the door and hopped out of the vehicle, before holding it open for her. The two black horses pulling the carriage looked similar to the ones from the other day, however, he could not be certain. The carriage was different.

How curious. Why is she stalking me like a stricken deer? And how did she know I would be here, unless she had someone to tell her? His mind turned over and over everything he remembered from White's. His careless accident had brought undue attention his way, so he could not be sure who was the informant. He rolled up his sleeves and stepped into the ring determined to focus his attention on his boxing, lest he end up on his back.

Two hours later, emerging from the boxing saloon, Harlow squinted up at the sun.

"Thank you, my friend. You have performed a valiant service," he said, wiping the sweat from his brow. "I confess I found it hard to concentrate. Lady Poinz's appearance weighed heavily on my mind."

"That could explain the bruise you gave me with your uppercut," Max guffawed good-naturedly. "I thought faces were without one's bounds."

"My aim was for your shoulder. You ducked and caught my fist." Harlow replied cheerfully. "On a serious note, I would like to find out the name of the man with whom Lady Poinz rode in that carriage. How did she know to look for me here? And, indeed, why was she doing so? Was she following one of us, or both of us? I have several questions," he contended.

"Those are very good questions. I would also like to discover the man's identity. It could be connected with our investigation."

"There are quite a few loose ends. I will have Dean discreetly look into Lady Poinz's investments. As my man of business, he should know who to ask," Harlow stressed.

"We need to discover her recent dealings and try to determine her motive. I teased you earlier, but this could be serious. Let me see what I may learn at Headquarters before we leave tomorrow," Max proposed. "If she has her claws into you for some reason, then you may need to be careful with whom you associate."

Lady Lilian. Harlow's breath caught in his throat.

CHAPTER 9

The next morning, the house buzzed with activity.

"Pardon me, m'lady. I have your chocolate and biscuits here. Would you like me to pack the books ye have laid out on your table?" The maid moved into the room with a tray and tipped her head towards the books.

"Thank you, Mary. Yes, put them in the bottom of my valise, please." Lilian glanced out of the window at the street, feeling discouraged. It was a beautiful, late summer day without clouds in the sky, something that London rarely experienced. She would normally feel blissful at the sight. It seemed as if the last several years had been cloudier and chillier, so a cloudless sky should feel inspiring. Instead, she felt bereft. There had been no word from Lord Harlow—John—in three days and she chided herself for allowing herself to think there had been some affinity between them. Yet something tugged at her heart…hope, maybe?

A small bark from the doorway grabbed her attention. "Cooper! There you are, my little one. I have something for you." Lilian lifted up her pillow and pulled out the fabric ball she had made for her puppy. She had carefully taken old sheeting and wrapped it over discarded paper stuffing that she had already secured in some of Father's discarded news sheets, sewing the fabric down until she formed a perfect ball shape. She had noticed Cooper's affection for playing ball and had decided he needed a larger one that he could chase, thinking it would be easier to see and retrieve for him. He would get it dirty, but she would worry about that later.

At the sight of the ball, the little puppy stood up on his hind-legs and balancing, yapped in hopeful delight. *Surely, he has never had one of these toys, but he knows it is for him.*

"You are such a keen puppy, Cooper." Lilian tossed the ball out of the door of her room, towards the wall opposite, and he ran after it. A minute later, he returned, holding it in his teeth and spinning his tail around. His tail wagged in a circular motion. "Oh, good gracious, your tail twirls around when you are as happy as this!" Pleased with his reaction, she laughed and clapped as Cooper's tail continued to whirl.

"M'lady, I don't think as I have ever seen a dog wag 'is tail like that," Mary remarked, pausing while packing books. "A true treasure ye have there, m'lady."

"He brings a smile to my lips." This little dog lifted her heart. "I dare not consider what he has been through." She called Cooper to her side and lifted him to her lap, ball and all. They had already this morning bathed his neck with vinegar and applied the tincture to it. She lifted the thin band of sheeting which loosely covered his injuries. "They look much better today, Cooper. You will be as good as new in another day or so. Mr. Whitten did a good job." She fleetingly wondered if he enjoyed working with animals. He must do, she decided, as it could be both a cheering and disheartening task. She tugged on the blue velvet bell-pull near the settee to summon help and Winston arrived with Clara bustling behind.

The tall, broad-shouldered footman waited while Clara

scurried about, grabbing Cooper's basket, pillow and his little blue ball.

"I declare, the young master is already leaving his things about," she chuckled. "I was on my way 'ere to tell you, m'lady. Ye 'ave company in the parlour," Clara whispered, winking in a familiar fashion which Lilian ignored.

"A visitor? I did not see anyone arrive. How unusual." Casting off her earlier low spirits, she picked up the book she was reading and nodded her head, signalling to Winston she was ready. He carried her downstairs, with Cooper running ahead, hugging the wall and holding his new ball between his teeth—tail spinning in circles behind him. Clara followed everyone. She usually did so in case Lilian dropped something.

"Yer dog has a fancy tail, m'lady," Winston remarked lightly as they made their way down the second flight of stairs. "I am sure as I have never seen a tail spin around on a dog before."

"He is entertaining, Winston, and a hearty encouragement in my life. He makes me smile." Winston rarely spoke, except brief words. Cooper was affecting everyone's mood.

Winston placed her in the chair and released the brake. Clara walked up from behind and pushed the chair in the parlour's direction. The yellow floral paper on the hall walls cast the area in a happy light, elevating her mood further as they passed into the parlour. At her entrance a tall, brown-haired man handed his coat to Chambers and turned around, smiling. He was holding a posy of forget-me-knots.

"These are for you, my lady." Harlow offered the flowers to Lilian, his eyes glittering with some kind of emotion she could not decipher. "I would have come yesterday, but business kept me away. It is my fondest hope that you will forgive me that oversight."

Lilian was not sure what to say. She had missed him. Briefly, she considered telling him so, but pride kept her from revealing her feelings.

"These are lovely, my lord..."

"John," he murmured for her ears alone. Clara had taken her needlework and was sitting behind him in the striped chair.

"Ooh!" she exclaimed, sucking her finger. "Do, please excuse me, m'lord, m'lady. I must attend to this before the blood ruins my piece." She jumped up from the chair and moved past them in a hurry.

"It seems we have the room to ourselves for a moment," he responded.

"Yes...but if you think to importune me, sir, Chambers will be nearby, in the hall." She turned and looked at him, hoping her eyes and tone gave the lie to her words as she whispered her response.

"Never would I—!" he began, before his frown lifted and he continued, "Would you enjoy a turn in the garden? I have a question to ask." He ventured forward, tilting her chin up to him with his index finger. "Forgive me if I worried you; if you thought I would not be back. I had not considered your feelings enough in my absence."

She stared down at the flowers, needing to hide the tears which threatened. Thinking they were gone, she looked up at him again.

"No, John," she whispered. "I have been occupied," she lied. A lump rose in her throat as she spoke. *Yes, I spent the days worrying I would not see you again. I cannot tell you that, of course.* Involuntarily, she sniffled. "I should thank you, sir, for sending Mr. Whitten. He made a friend in Cooper." Somehow, she managed a short laugh. "He examined him all over and left us some medicines to help with his injuries."

"Mr. Whitten is a good friend of mine. We met while fighting in France. His experience in animal science helped immensely with our horses. He assisted the regiment's veterinary surgeon and kept many of us mounted, as he was quick to spot difficulties. Another friend of mine, a doctor, introduced us. Lord Maxwell Wilde, the Earl of Worsley, was present and the four of us remain as close as brothers.

Harlow reached out and touched her hands lightly, causing her stomach to flip.

"I am sorry to have neglected you, Lilian. I wish I could make amends for that." He gave her free hand a light squeeze.

She recognized Clara's footsteps approaching along the hall and pulled back. *Drat! I could smell him, he was so close.* Dangerously *close.* She shivered.

John stepped back as well, setting them at a proper distance just before Clara reappeared.

"Did ye tell his lordship we are leaving for Tintagel in an hour?" Clara could be impertinent, owing to the considerable licence she enjoyed with the family. Now Lilian suddenly understood all too well her mother's difficulty with Clara's effrontery and was forced to inhale a deep, calming breath.

"Clara, his lordship has asked me to take a turn about the garden with him. We will be in the rose gardens, should anyone ask. Cooper will act as my chaperone." At that moment, Cooper walked in, presenting a comical sight. The dog's teeth firmly gripped the large ball, which banged against his paws on the left side of his body, dragging and impeding his gait.

Harlow roared with genuine laughter. "He is barely bigger than his new ball—which reminds me..." Breaking off, John reached into his pocket and withdrew a smaller red ball, securing it in Lilian's palm. "He may enjoy this. I recall that dogs enjoy sport."

"Yes, he loves playing with a ball." She chuckled. "Mama recognized that very quickly. She gave Cooper a ball with a blue tether attached so that I could throw it and retrieve it. Cooper enjoys himself immensely." Lilian loved her dog. How quickly that had happened, she reflected. *I do not want to discuss Cooper. I want to know more about him...about the two of us. Could we be a twosome?* She realized she wanted them to be a twosome.

They opened the side door of the morning room and moved outside onto a small, stoned courtyard. A row of still-green Camellia bushes added an element of privacy to the area. A large elm tree provided shade, while a carpet of bright green moss grew from the bottom of the tree and extended to the lawn, where the sun broke through the leaves. Red and yellow rose bushes lined a stone walk which led to a small white gazebo covered with the foliage of a jasmine that had long since bloomed, which stood behind carpets of pink asters, purple verbena and white daisies.

"This is beautiful," Harlow whispered close to her ear. "You have a very insightful gardener."

His breath sent delicious shivers down her spine. "It is my mother's passion, mostly. Williams does the heavier work, but you can frequently find my mother out here, wearing a large hat and gardening gloves. She says it is her way of painting." She pointed ahead. "Would you like to sit in the gazebo? Mama had a small ramp attached to it so I might easily gain access to it. I love to read out here." Lilian could smell his fragrance of bergamot and bay leaf, even amongst the blooms, and inhaled quietly. She enjoyed his nearness as much as she feared it would be short-lived. They were leaving.

Harlow pushed her chair into place beside the small iron one in the gazebo and turned her towards him.

"I have a few things I would like to say, if you will allow it."

She did not want to hear bad news. She nodded her head quietly, steeling her insides for what he might say.

"I must leave Town for the Cornwall coast tomorrow, to hopefully conclude some business. I had hoped you might be willing to continue allowing me to court you." His throat worked, but he said no more.

Her pulse quickened. "When will you be leaving?" She swallowed, struggling to control her excitement.

"Would you mind if I sat next to you?" he asked.

"Not at all." She clasped her hands in front of her and glanced around, spotting Cooper chasing a butterfly behind the elm tree. Her throat pulsed wildly. The window to her father's study opened to the garden, and she speculated if he was in there, but the curtains were closed. She imagined he had drawn them yesterday to keep the sun from overheating the room. This morning he had escorted Mama and Lydia into Town to purchase last-minute items for their journey back to Tintagel, and she had not heard them return.

"May I kiss you? I have so much to discuss with you, but while we have a moment alone, I would like to kiss you. We may only have a moment before your maid appears."

Kiss me? The question startled her back to reality. "Yes," she breathed, placing her hand over her fluttery stomach. Absently, she wondered how this could be achieved from her wheel-chair. Impulsively, she shuttered her eyes.

Harlow moved closer and slipped one arm around her, pulling her nearer. She felt his hand slip into her hair, gently moving his fingers among the curls hanging at the back of her neck. His lips touched hers, tenderly at first, then with more pressure, with his tongue teasing her lips to open.

Lilian enjoyed his kiss and leaned further into his caress,

yielding to the pressure of his mouth. His tongue swiftly entered, parrying and dancing with her own as it explored the recesses of her mouth and stirred up tingling, strange feelings in the very centre of her body, compelling her to want more—of what, she was not sure. However, she knew she did not want this kiss to end.

A small bark from the corner of the garden brought them back from the heavens, alerting them to visitors, and they pulled apart, both breathing heavily. Cooper barked again, and Lilian saw Clara come through the door from the house and take the bench in the stoned courtyard.

"I believe we have a champion in that little dog," Harlow observed. "Thank you. I enjoyed that kiss."

"I enjoyed it too," she said shyly. "I confess I would have liked it to last a moment longer..." She stopped then, suddenly realizing the lack of propriety in her words and behaviour. Whatever was she about, to be enjoying stolen minutes alone with him and a kiss that had singed her to her core. What must he be thinking? She was little better than... than a bird of paradise!

"Lilian, you are the first woman I have courted in a very long time. I fear I need to dust off my rules of etiquette!" He tried to appear apologetic and failing, laughed instead.

"Oh...are there written rules for gentlemen, too?" A gurgle of laughter escaped her throat. "I am truly sorry," she excused herself quickly, lifting a hand to her mouth. "I did not mean to offend—I suddenly visualized a book of rules gentlemen must follow in order to court a lady. It struck me as funny. I apologize."

"There is no need to apologize. There are rules, ah...principles, if you will. For example, as boys, our tutors teach us we must be honest, be prompt, even early...that type of thing. My father showed me a book and asked that I read it. I think

I may still have it." He sat back in his chair and laughed. "I have not thought about that book in years. I believe it was called something like, 'The Gentlemen Instructed…' He stopped. "There was more to the title, but it escapes me. Anyway, I am endeavouring to adhere to those teachings."

"In what way are you falling short, John?" Lilian watched his lips as he spoke to her. His lips were perfect, not too thin and not too full. She wanted to feel them again.

"I have not wanted to get married because I have bad dreams." He rushed the words forth, his eyes fixed on her.

"What kinds of dreams?" she ventured cautiously, grasping her hands to her heart.

"Ever since the war, I wake up sweating, sometimes screaming. I am sure I have no notion why I am telling you this. It seems most unseemly to be discussing such a thing, yet, I fear to mislead you. I feel I can trust you and tell you this about me, not knowing for sure where our…connection…will lead."

Lilian became quiet and folded her hands into her lap. "Thank you for sharing that. It could not have been easy. In fact, I cannot imagine my brother talking about such matters, even with my mother or father." She looked up at him, carefully taking her hand and caressing the side of his face. "You can trust that I will never speak of this to anyone. I will not marry unless there is love or the chance of love. I would rather not marry if I have no feeling for a gentleman," she spoke softly, almost whispering.

"My parents were a love match, but Mother seems to have put that aside in her concern for an heir. She wants grandchildren, and I can understand that."

Lilian dipped her head slightly in acknowledgement. She had no idea how else to respond. Her doctor had not indicated any concerns with having children, and until now, she had given no thought to courtship in the past year.

"So, are we agreed? We will seek to become better acquainted and see what may develop, both agreeing to tell the other if we find it too difficult or that we do not suit after all? He fixed his eyes on her face.

Her throat suddenly felt parched. All she could do was nod.

"It is time we returned to the house. Clara has twice risen to her feet, I think perhaps she is giving us a hint." He stood up and looked down at her. "I will call upon you when we are arrived in Cornwall. I leave tomorrow morning with Lord Worsley." He leaned down to kiss her head and she looked up, catching his lips on her nose. He leaned in and brushed her lips. "To brand you mine until we see each other in Tintagel."

Footfalls on loose gravel sounded beyond the gazebo. Stepping behind her chair, Harlow quickly began pushing it back toward the house.

"Clara, I will escort Lady Lilian into the house and then I shall take my leave before I offend all the tenets of propriety."

"M'lord. Lord and Lady Avalon are returned. We will be leaving shortly." Clara stopped and gasped. "M'lord, a man moved from behind the pink rosebushes." She pointed to the rosebush-covered fence line that stood in front of the alley that led to the mews.

Harlow ran to the fence and looked, then came back with a dismissive look on his face. "I only saw a groom carrying a bucket of oats to the carriage horses, Clara," he said, gripping the back of Lilian's chair.

Lilian was propelled into the house with her hands in her lap but her head in the clouds. She was unsure what had just happened, except that she had agreed to put her heart at risk. Her heart was bursting with more hope than she had felt in a year.

~

A few minutes later, a short, moustached man stepped out from behind the mews of Avalon House and walked back towards the road where his dappled grey horse waited.

CHAPTER 10

Guilt assailed him as he rode home. Harlow suspected Lilian could be in danger, but it was only an instinctive sense. He had no evidence. There had been no threats, but he trusted his gut. Staying near her was not an obligation; he wanted to stay near her. She made him laugh and she challenged him with her wit and interest in any topic, and her willingness to listen and hear past the spoken word. Then there was that kiss... Harlow touched his lips and could have sworn the feel of her still lingered on his lips. Her lips were soft, and her rose-water scent had imprinted itself in his mind.

Aware he could not share his commission with anyone, Harlow tried to think of every way he could keep his activities secret and still protect Lady Lilian and her family. He thought of her father. Lord Avalon should be informed of any progress. He would provide that when they arrived in Tintagel. Harlow wanted to believe that Tintagel was a safe distance, but the smugglers he was after had proven their hearts to be black and he would not leave Lilian's safety to chance.

Harlow arrived at his town house and handed his horse's reins to his groom. Intent on getting to his study, he ran to the front door, nearly knocking down Fitz, his butler.

"My lord," Fitz pronounced in stringent tones as he stepped aside, "I trust your afternoon was tolerable."

"It was pleasant enough." Fitz must be losing his hearing. His tone was more like a bellow than a calm remark. The corpulent retainer had been with the family as long as Harlow could remember.

"Very good, my lord. Lord Worsley awaits you in the study," the stout, balding man piercingly declared to his back.

"Thank you, Fitz." Harlow handed his hat, gloves and cane to the butler and headed down the dark-panelled hall to the open doorway of his study, which was still filled with the early morning sunshine.

The servant accompanied Harlow to his sanctum. "That will be all, Fitz."

"Of course, my lord." The older man bowed and closed the doors to the study behind him.

"I had just gotten in the door when I heard you arrive, riding like the hounds of hell were upon you." Max discarded his waistcoat to the chair beside him and made himself more comfortable. "You still seem out of sorts. I took the liberty of pouring you a whisky. Your cook waited upon me soon after I arrived and said she has orders to serve a nuncheon in here. It seems convenient because I believe we have a great deal to discuss."

"I need do nothing; my household functions without me," Harlow mused aloud. "You make an exceeding efficient housekeeper, my friend." He downed the brandy in a single gulp and threw himself into a chair. "In case you are wondering, I did it," he said, putting down the glass which, by some miracle, had survived intact.

"Did *it*? I do not understand the significance of 'it'." Max emphasized the last word. "You would rather I not have a brandy awaiting your arrival?" He gave a sardonic smile and took another sip from his own glass.

"Of course, I want a brandy waiting for me." Harlow laughed nervously. "I told her about my dreams." He rose and poured himself another brandy.

"Did she leave the room and hide?" Max chuckled caustically.

"It is hard to comprehend. However, she did not leave. I almost ran. I have feelings for her, yet I am not sure I can marry. The worst about all of this, is I believe our initial inquiries made in her community may have accidentally rendered her the target for a bullet meant for one of us. Her whole life was destroyed that day." Harlow choked on the pain and fear that flooded his being as he spoke.

"That is something I had not considered before. It is a lot of guilt you are carrying on your shoulders, my friend," Max remarked soberly.

Harlow nodded and walked to the fireplace, which stood between two ceiling-high spans of shelving and dominated the wall. Leaning his head against the wooden mantel, he looked down at his feet.

"It has weighed on me all year. Now, to see her confined to a wheel-chair…it renewed the burden—brought back all that happened."

"Are you seeing her because of the guilt?" Max's tone was harsh.

"No! Of course not." A flash of temper hit his eyes. "There is something special about her. She has no guile. Lilian ushers light into what is a very dark world, especially given the amount of death we have seen." He kept his head down this time and nursed his whisky, unwilling to allow Max to read his face again—because he had lied…a little. The truth was, at least at first, he had wanted to meet her out of guilt. The rest, however, was honest. *I have feelings. I just did not understand them. It is like nothing I have experienced before; a lightness of the heart.*

"Do you feel Lord Avalon holds you responsible? He knows of our commission." Max's tone was critical.

"No. I doubt it." Harlow walked to his window and stared at the small veranda his mother had built years ago. "Max, you have known me for a long time. Give me a little credit." His voice strained. He turned and glared at his friend, no longer concerned about being questioned. "And no, I have said nothing to Lord Avalon of my suspicions. Do but consider, Max," he implored. "The gunshot. Recall we had just come from nosing about the town. We could have been discovered. That was all there was until the day of the ball. The widow made her appearance—no one on her arm, and no real purpose…but she noticed my attention towards Lady Lilian. Add that to what we discussed yesterday—her connections to the alehouses and…"

"We suspect her, but we do not have direct evidence. Only questions."

"I think we probably should talk to Avalon," Harlow muttered.

"That is risking a great deal, Harlow." Max's tone was no longer tinged with misgivings. "I say we go to the coast with all speed, take a look around and then decide. Let us give ourselves two days to formulate a plan of action…"

"With one caveat," Harlow interjected. "If we see anything that indicates that the two sisters could be in danger, we let their father know."

"Agreed."

"What news do you have of the missing boat of Revenue men?" Harlow moved to sit behind his desk and leaned forward, hands clasped.

"They found the riding officers…all six of them…dead. The boat was floating off the coast of Cornwall. A British man of war spotted it. The Home Office wants the person or persons responsible to hang for this. They need us to get this situation under control. We have been investigating it for almost a year, with only small successes. I do not feel I am ready to name the chief suspect—yet." Max's tone was sober. "Prinny is sending an agent, someone who has experience inside the smuggling trade, to meet with us. The only name they provided was John Cressey. We are to meet him at the Anchor's Away Public House on Boswell Street at four of the clock. He will approach us and ask to share our table."

"Sounds cryptic. However, the name is familiar to me." Harlow was pouring himself another whisky when the door opened, and a footman brought in a tray full of soup and sandwiches. "This should help us think. I cannot conjecture where I have heard that name before, but I recognize it." He motioned for the footman to put the food on the game table near the fireplace.

"Of course, my lord. Will there be anything else?" the footman inquired.

"No, thank you, Wells." Harlow nodded appreciation.

The two men took their glasses and seated themselves at the table as the footman left the room, pulling the study's heavy wooden door closed behind him.

"Someone has to be operating from the inside. No one could be as auspicious as they have been without help. They know when the big shipments are coming—which ships have prime cargo. Those are the ships picked off by whoever this is." Harlow drained his glass. "Pass me that decanter, friend. I believe I need more."

"You are besotted," Max quietly observed. "The Harlow I know is much calmer than this. I know you for your coolness under pressure. You are like to become foxed if you keep swilling the juice in this fashion."

"Yes. I am noted for my self-possession. I am afraid I walked into this association with my eyes wide open. It was as if I could not control myself. She draws me to her like a moth to a flame." Harlow smiled to himself and swirled the last vestiges of his drink around in the glass before swallowing it. He glanced at the silver tray still sitting on a small stand next to the table. "Excellent! Wells brought a pot of tea. So, you see, I will not succumb to my potations."

"Your cook is excellent," Max said, pouring himself a cup of hot tea. "I will have tea for now." He toasted Harlow. "I have not had turtle soup this good in many a year."

"Would you mind if we again turn our attention to the smuggling?" Harlow put down his glass.

"Apparently, Cressey is already immersed into the smuggling trade and was key to taking down, a few months ago, that major gun and ammunitions organization which was trading to the French. He will send us a message with a meeting place. We are to meet him this afternoon before we leave for Cornwall." Max wiped his mouth. "I notice you have not touched your soup. If you do not want it, I will eat it. I slept late this morning and am just now breaking my fast," he offered.

"It would be unusual if either of us left a single snack." Harlow laughed, reaching for a warm roll and smearing butter on it. "We know several of those involved in the Tintagel smuggling ring, just not the leader, and we need to determine who on the inside is providing their information. As you are aware, they only attack certain boats and seem to know exactly the ones to take. Thus, they must have an informant," he added, shifting back to the subject at hand.

"The Prince Regent is most interested in this matter since the murder of the six tax assessors. While he has been known to enjoy smuggled French brandy, himself, one of the men was a particular friend of Prinny's, if you get my meaning," Max put in as he finished the soup.

"I had heard something of that. From what I understand, Cressey operated as an intelligencer, and Prinny has asked that he lend his services from within the thieves' network." Harlow put down his napkin. "The meeting is set for this afternoon, we need to stir ourselves."

An hour later, they were approaching the public house where Harlow had seen the black coach when the heavy, blackened oak door opened and a tall, burly man tossed a drunkard into the street.

"'Oi don't want to see yer scrawny arse back in 'ere again," the owner shouted after the man landed in the gutter. Max and Harlow stepped around the sprawled man and entered the tavern. The room was dank and dark. It took a moment for Harlow's eyes to adjust to the light.

"I see an empty table at the very back, away from the window and the bar. We will take that, two mugs of beer, and a small plate of cheese and salted meats," Harlow directed the sparsely dressed barmaid who met them at the door. Max sat against the back wall and Harlow took a seat to his right, giving both men a good view of the alehouse's door.

"'Ave anything else, your lordships?" she asked, brazenly staring at Harlow's lap before turning and sashaying towards the kitchen with their order.

"I think the convenient fancies you, bully-boy!" Max remarked when her back was to them.

"I would not fancy her or her added incentives, even if I were ape-drunk," countered Harlow. "Hush." He gave a slight nod towards the kitchen. "She is returning with our repast."

The slattern duly dumped two foaming tankards and a plate of viands on the table in front of them and sniffed, pointedly swinging her hips as she walked away.

"I think, mayhap, she heard you," Max remarked. Harlow ignored him and lifted one of the tankards.

A few minutes later, a man dressed in black entered the tavern. He quickly scanned the room and then moved towards Harlow's table.

"Friends, would you mind if I shared your table?" he asked, looking both of them in the eye.

"Certainly." Harlow signalled to the barmaid to bring beer for their guest.

"'Ere you go, guvnor," she returned, setting the glass of ale on the table and leaning down as low as she could, barely keeping her breasts in her blouse as she set the glass on the table.

Harlow flipped her a shilling and thanked her, hoping she would take her wares to the other side of the room.

"There is no telling what other…attractions come with those wares she offers," he said in a low voice, involuntarily shivering at the thought. "We are finally alone." He turned to the bearded man. "You are…" he began to say but was brought up short when the bearded man quietly put up his hand. "…arrogant," he finished under his breath.

"I realize my beard fools neither of you. When we leave here tonight, and until this commission is over, you know me only as John Cressey." Laughter erupted from behind him at that moment and DeLacey turned his head defensively.

"Did you think they were laughing at your beard?" Max quipped, leaning back in his seat and eyeing the man. "They were laughing because the barmaid serving the ape-drunk man near the door lost her tit into his glass of ale, and he tried to claim it."

Harlow nearly choked on his beer. Jonathan DeLacey enjoyed banter as much as anyone. However, he nurtured a larger measure of himself than most and found being the object of ridicule difficult. His ego made him an easy target and had evoked much hilarity at school. The problem was, school was ten years ago. This was dangerous business they ventured into today, and his ego could get them all killed.

"Damn, I thought...never mind." DeLacey took a deep breath.

Harlow leaned forward. "Stubble it, Cressey. You thought they were laughing at you. If they were, we would have taken measure of it and perhaps joined in, if it served our purpose. Put your ego away and there will be less risk to all our lives."

DeLacey stared at Harlow. For a long moment, no one spoke. Finally, he nodded. "I will endeavour not to react when being the butt of someone's wit. I realise my appearance surprised you. I grow a beard when I am operating as Cressey."

"Your father, does he know?" Harlow followed his own query with a statement, putting forth the question that had been burning in his mind. "He is part of it, too." It was common for the Home Office to keep secret the identity of those working for them, even within the ranks.

"We respect that... and the beard is not too dreadful." Max smirked. "We need to protect ourselves, and it helps that we know each other," he spoke softly, and all three nodded.

"Your family has gone to Tintagel. I am surprised that you did not go also," Harlow ventured, suddenly irritated that Lilian's brother was not there to safeguard her. He reminded himself his fear was his own speculation. It added to his anxiety to set off for the coast.

"I leave for Tintagel tonight, but this commission keeps me away from home. However, I trust that they are safe enough. I cannot fathom any involvement on their part," he spoke slowly, eyeing Harlow.

Harlow heated under his old schoolfellow's scrutiny but maintained a calm demeanour. *He suspects.* Harlow stalled for the right answer and regarded the room around him. Two oil lanterns hanging from the ramparts barely provided adequate lighting, casting shadows onto dingy blue walls. A group of locals and sailors sat on chairs, using a bench between them as a table between them for a rowdy card game. Behind them, a man lay asleep on the bench beneath the table. Cigar smoke circled the heads of patrons, only adding to the sour stench of retched ale long since dried on the floor.

"It appears we have a few matters to discuss before we get down to business," he said finally, keeping his emotions in check. "I believe the bullet that almost claimed your sister's life was meant for us, but it is mere speculation since we had been frequenting the area while observing."

DeLacey arched a brow. "It has been my belief as well, and until you began courting her, I had thought Lilian safe from any further injury. What are your intentions towards my sister?"

DeLacey's question caught him unawares. While Harlow was prepared to discuss his suspicions, he was not, however, ready for that.

"It should please you to know that I laid out my intentions before Lilian yesterday," he said, thinking he could evade further discussion.

"Meaning?"

The man is not going to let this drop. Harlow took a deep breath, then glanced at Max, who sat emotionless. Apparently, he was willing to hear Harlow out, as well.

"Lady Lilian and I discussed pursuing our acquaintance in order to determine the depth of our feelings for each other." He paused to clear an uncomfortable lump in his throat. "I have avoided marriage thus far, primarily because I have..." He struggled for the word. "...I have episodes at night which I do not wish to subject a wife to, and I explained that. Despite this obvious drawback, I find in myself a desire to court her."

"My sister is comfortable with that?" DeLacey responded in a surprised tone.

"Yes, she indicated she was, but it is my full intention to establish if we suit. I have feelings for her." Saying it aloud to her brother made it, all at once, seem very real, he realized, hoping the sudden sweat on his brow would remain hidden in this dank setting.

"Very well, but you had better maintain those honourable intentions. I would expect no less of you," DeLacey whispered. "However, toy with my sister's feelings, and I will call you out."

"He has the same nightmares many of us brought home from the war," Max spoke up quietly. "Your sentiments are understandable, but we both know he would never toy with an innocent. Now, do we get to business and dispense with this. Tell us what you already know."

Now you speak up, Max. Where were you a few moments ago? He wanted to fume, but Harlow found it hard to be annoyed with either man. Both were protecting Lilian's interests. *She did not react to the news of my nightmares.* He clung to the hope that Lilian would be perfect for him. Shaking his head slightly, he attempted to clear her from his mind.

"I believe the entire operation emanates from Tintagel and is run by someone with multiple business interests…" DeLacey passed on his knowledge. "The town apparently knows and supports this man, although I do not think he lives there…"

"It is a woman, we think," Max cut in softly. "We believe her to be the widow Poinz."

"Lud!" DeLacey grew quiet. "The *ton* knows her only for her temper and her jealousies, not to mention her wealth since her husband died. It could fit."

"His death is still a mystery," added Max, as he popped a piece of salted meat into his mouth.

"Yes, it is." DeLacey sipped his ale. "It makes sense. She owns public houses and inns across the Cornish coast and into England. Indeed, we had not ruled out a woman, upon the stock of something we heard from an informer."

"Did the informer tell you anything about their signals?" Harlow asked.

"No, but I have my suspicions. The entire community profits from their activities and they all look the other way. However, I have noticed a few things," DeLacey added. He leaned closer. "If you think the widow leads, that is key information and will help us determine who is on the inside. It will be someone she is close to…in the government." He passed a list of names to the two men and waited for them to look at it.

"There is not much light, but I recognize many of these names," Max said, angling the list slightly to catch the meagre light from a lamp hanging nearby.

"They are names given to me by an unwilling informant. Watch for a farmer on a white horse. I think he is part of the signal. I believe he signals with it," DeLacey acknowledged. DeLacey reached out for the list and shredded it into small pieces, stuffing the pieces in his pocket.

"We have noticed him. He rides his horse to town, and either walks back, leading the horse along the main road, or returns by riding it along the coast road. We think the latter is an all-clear signal as it has coincided with ships being wrecked. We could have called the Dragoons and pulled in the net, but we need the conspirator from within," Harlow spoke very low, although given the hum of conversation, it was unlikely they would be overheard.

Max and DeLacey nodded and finished their ale. "I have a suggestion for a dropping place," DeLacey broke the silent comradeship, his voice also low. "It should be easy enough to do. There is a loose cornerstone, low to the ground, on the north corner—back facing side—of the post office. The stone is grey and sits among two badly chipped white ones. The building does not get busy until about ten of the clock. Put your messages there." He laid his palms down on the table. "I will leave first. And I will be in contact."

"Agreed."

CHAPTER 11

Five days later.

Lilian's body jostled in the coach as it rolled across the uneven stone paving on Bossiney Road, taking them through the small coastal town of Tintagel. Five days in a coach had challenged the adults, but Cooper seemed to enjoy the attention. Remarkably, the puppy could conduct his business at main stops and added no strain to the trip. His presence lightened her mood considerably, although she thought more and more about the handsome Lord Harlow, wishing she had been a little more forward and kissed him again, having never been kissed before then. It seemed an age since they had left for London, and she wondered when she would see Lord Harlow again. He had shown an interest in continuing their courtship, she told herself. *I will make sure to receive another kiss on his next visit.* She found herself daydreaming about his last kiss.

Sitting for hours exhausted everyone, and even her books

had begun to bore her. "It has been so long since I have seen Darby," she murmured to herself. "I wonder how he will get on with Cooper," she added, stroking the small dog in her lap.

"I suspect they will enjoy each other's company. Danby enjoys running loose in the pasture. Cooper enjoys chasing and seems agile. When the puppy grows, he might keep up with your horse." Lydia leaned over and tickled Cooper behind the ear.

"I apologize. I had not realized I had spoken my thoughts aloud." Heat rose as she wondered if that was all she had uttered. Leaning down, Lilian gave Cooper a quick kiss on his head. "You will enjoy chasing Danby, little man," she told him. "Danby has been with me a little longer, so you may have to give him time to get used to sharing. However, I think the two of you could be the best of friends." She propped back and closed her eyes, conjuring up Elysium Manor. The drive to her home wound around a small lake, two-thirds of the edge of which was framed by an apple orchard. The scenery always brought to mind images her grandmama had given her in stories she had told her years ago.

According to legend, Avalon was the place they took King Arthur to recover after the Battle of Camlann. Grandmama had explained that Grandpapa had loved hearing stories of King Arthur when he was growing up and so he had renamed the property Elysium Manor because it gave a mystical aura to the name, and because the meaning of Avalon was very much the same as Elysium. Elysium had sounded more magical to him. Avalon and Elysium both meaning *isle of apples*, Grandpapa had planted large tracts of apple trees along the far side of the lake. It had been her favourite place to ride while growing up, especially during the summer. Danby had favoured being allowed to reach an occasional apple, which were always plentiful in the summer, from the trees.

She could tell when their black carriage pulled off the road and onto the drive leading to Elysium Manor, and heaved a sigh. *We are almost home. Just ten more minutes.* She heard the oyster shells that covered the road being crushed beneath the carriage. Mama instructed the servants to always crush and spread any crustacean shells whenever they served seafood. That had been a family custom, and it added a fashionable appeal. Over the years, the drive had become mostly shells, until it ended at the circular brick drive in front of the house. On impulse, Lilian moved the curtain aside to look. The house stood on a slight hill in front of them. The pink brick and grey limestone, Georgian-styled manor had large east and west wings of three storeys, while the main house was four storeys. Matching brick paved a large round drive in front of the house.

Her family's three carriages came to a stop, the massive oak door opened, and the housekeeper and footman greeted them. Chambers always travelled to London when they opened up the town house, but the home journey taxed him immensely because he could not reach his post quickly enough. She knew Chambers and Clara well enough to know they would be supervising everything in a matter of minutes, the very moment their feet touched the ground. As if he heard her thoughts, Chambers took his habitual position at the door, causing the housekeeper and footman to withdraw.

"My lord, Lady Avalon, ladies, welcome home!" The stout man pulled on his waistcoat as if shaking out any residual wrinkles.

"Thank you, Chambers. You did not have to rush to greet us. You have just arrived home yourself," declared Father, as he exited the conveyance.

Lilian was always last. She imagined Winston was

bringing the chair they maintained here to the door. He would carry her up the steps. She found no enjoyment in this part of her homecoming.

It was still early in the day and Lilian was most eager to see her horse. "Would you go to the stables with me, Lydia? Cooper should meet his bigger brother."

"*Brother*, you say? Lud! Danby is a *horse* and you are not his *mother*." Lydia pretended exasperation.

"Will you go with me? I am quite excited to be home again." Lilian knew Lydia would go with her.

"Let me change my dress first. I am most eager to get this dusty gown off!" Lydia responded.

An hour later, Lilian wheeled her chair down a newly bricked path to the stables. Father had arranged for the completion of this while in London. Lilian was delighted at the surprise. It made access to her horse so much easier. The new gardens thrilled Cooper. He walked ahead of her, stopping every few minutes to assure himself she was behind him. He sniffed everything—dandelions, grass, trees, bushes, everything, and marked as much as possible as his territory. Lilian smiled at his antics while she wheeled herself down the path. It took a little longer than being pushed; however, the path had a slight downward slope from the house, so she moved unimpeded. *Returning to the house will require some help*, she thought.

"Good afternoon, m'lady," called Barney, surprise clear on his face. He dusted off his hands, walked up and pushed her towards the stable yard. "I know who ye are 'ere to see. 'E will be mighty glad to see you, m'lady. I've put him in the Long Meadow."

"Oh, I hope so! I have brought him a bag of apple slices from the kitchen." Lilian pulled one out of her pocket.

"We have been enjoying the apples your grandpapa

planted. 'Tis a good season for them this year. Cook has already made several pies."

"They are my favourite pies," Lilian exclaimed. "I shall have a piece today, should there be any left!"

Barney turned her chair in front of the stables and wheeled it along the service road to one of the paddocks generally used for a mare with a new foal. "This is as close as I can bring you. Yer horse will be 'ere in a moment. I sent Ned to fetch 'im." Barney then nodded at Cooper, who raced up to her chair and leaped onto her lap. "Who might this little fellow be, m'lady?"

"This is Cooper," she gleefully told him. "I found him in Richmond Park." Lilian withdrew a handkerchief from her pocket and unwrapped it, breaking a piece of the biscuit that Cook had given her. "Cooper, this is Barney." The little dog edged his nose into her other pocket and withdrew an apple slice from the bag and began to eat that.

"You like apples? I had not thought about that. Danby gets these, but we will not tell him.

"Ruff!" Cooper gave a quick bark. Barney gently patted the puppy on his head.

A shrill whinny pierced the air and a dark bay walked to the fence and leaned over, reaching her head, nickering softly in her ear.

"Danby! Lilian reached up and pulled him closer, kissing the stripe of white on his head. Cooper jumped off her lap, but stayed close to her, furiously sniffing the surrounding air. "He does not seem afraid of you, Danby."

Danby shook his head and nickered.

She scratched his face gently. "I hope that you will be friends. You are both dear to me."

"Ar-ruff!" A high-pitched bark alerted her and she turned her head.

"I tried to surprise you." Lydia laughed. "It looks as if I got here just in time for the grand meeting."

"Lydia, look at Cooper." Cooper had slowly moved to the fence and was making himself as tall as possible. His hackles were up and he was staring directly ahead. "No, Cooper." Danby stretched out his neck and nudged the puppy with his nose from under the fence. Cooper leaped backwards in the air and rolled over. Lilian reached down and picked up her puppy, putting him in her lap. "Oh, dear, that was funny, Cooper. My horse was just saying *good morning* to you. He is very handsome, is he not? See how his coat shines! We will have your coat as good as that soon." She withdrew the apple slices from her pocket. "Danby, I have something for you." Holding each slice in her palm, one by one she offered them to her horse. He took each sliver delicately and chewed it before coming back for the next.

"Ruff!" The puppy licked her nose and she gave him one.

"I see how this will be with you," Lilian said with a laugh, pulling the handkerchief open. "Here you go, little fellow," she said, feeding him the rest of his biscuit. She was glad to see that he no longer wolfed his food down. Instead, he accepted the food gently and seemed to enjoy it.

"I have something for you, too." Lydia pulled a walking stick out from behind her. "I had it made for you. I thought... well, never mind that. Here you are." She handed the stick to her sister.

Lilian looked at the cane. It was beautiful. The smooth mahogany cane held the head of a horse. A knot rose in her throat. *How could Lydia do this?*

"You know I cannot stand." She tried to say more, but her throat constricted.

"You have not tried to walk in a long time. Please, do consider it, Lilian. I think this will help you. You can stand here, with Danby and use the fence for more support. Your legs will work, I am convinced they will." Lydia peered down at Cooper. "I am counting on you to be a wonderful inspiration to my sister, little fellow."

"I do not know if I can do such a thing. The doctors…" Lilian's eyes blurred, and she could not finish her thought.

"The doctors said they did not understand why you could not walk. I have faith that you can. You do not have to try now." A single tear ran, unchecked, down Lydia's face. "I had two of them made for you. I thought I would leave this one near Danby. It can be kept by his stall, in case of need." Lydia smiled gently, wiping her face. "I believe you will walk again, Lilian."

Her sister believed her able to walk; Lilian knew her legs to be lifeless. Suddenly, she no longer felt enjoyment sitting beside the same paddock where she had learned to ride her first pony. She wanted to scream; she was frustrated and tired of this chair. Her sister's gift had touched her heart, but she felt anguished.

"I will try, later," she managed to answer with a semblance of civility. "Thank you, Lydia, for such a kind gift." Restlessness overwhelmed her. "Barney, please bring Danby into his stall. Perhaps I could sit near him and read for a while."

"Very good, m'lady." Barney stepped away from the fence and gathered Danby's halter from the gatepost where the stable-boy had left it.

"I feel as though I have spoilt the day for you, with my gift." Lydia gently squeezed Lilian's hand. "I will push you to the stables." She gave a short whistle. Lilian remembered their persuading Jonathan to teach them, one long-ago summer. "Follow us, Cooper." Lydia began pushing her sister's chair. "He is such a clever puppy." She duly propelled Lilian's chair into the stall next to Danby and positioned it so that her horse could reach her by leaning his head over the wall. "I will leave this, too," she added softly, placing the wooden cane near the wall. "It will be here when you are ready to try." She turned to leave just as Barney walked Danby into his stall.

"Will ye be needing your chestnut, m'lady?" Barney asked, his head craning around the partition to find Lilian. He gave a quick nod toward her new cane. "I will set a hook on the end 'ere, where it can do no 'arm, so as yer cane stays in the same spot for ye, Lady Lilian," he added.

"Thank you, Barney. No, I shall not be requiring Ginger today. Lilian, I must return to the house. Do not stay too long and take a chill. Mama said she had asked Cook to serve a light lunch and to tell you she expected you to join us."

"Thank you, Lydia." Lilian checked that the brake was set and then called for Cooper. The little dog had ventured around the partition but came running back when she whistled. She patted her lap, and he jumped into it. For a few long minutes, she looked around at the familiar sights. Her sister's mare usually stayed in the next stall. She thought about visiting Ginger as she was leaving but decided to let Cooper become better acquainted with Danby first. Reaching up, she fondled her horse's nose; he had, by then, turned from his manger and was leaning as far around the heel post as possible to whiffle at her. "Mind you do not get your legs caught in the chain, Danby, or Barney will put your headstall on. It seems that this will be a shorter visit than I had planned, but I will come again tomorrow and shall read to you.

There was a thud as something heavy fell off the wall at the entrance of the stable. Cooper began to bark, interspersing his barking with a strange whine.

"Stay," she directed Cooper, but he had already run off in the direction of the sound.

"I must see what that was, m'lady. I will be back in a moment." Barney hurried to investigate the noise and soon returned, carrying the small dog. The groom stood before her, looking puzzled and scratching his head. "'Twas strange. I have never known the lantern to fall off the wall afore. Lucky for us it were out, or we could have had a fire. I secured it back, but I shall check it again before I relight it. Yon dog seemed most distressed, m'lady. Kept jumping up and down like a flea…then he brought this piece of paper to me."

"May I see that?" She reached for the weathered piece of paper. It had writing on it, but it was so faded, she could not make out the letters. The letters she could decipher were either muddled from the weather or maybe smeared by the hand that wrote it. "I cannot make this out. Are you able to read anything?"

She waited for the groom to look. Barney shook his head, clearly distressed, and handed the note back to her. She remembered he did not know how to read, and her face burned at the realization of her thoughtlessness.

"It was fortuitous it happened in daylight when the lantern is unlit," she murmured aloud. An involuntary shudder shook her when she thought about what could have ensued. She was being foolish, she chastised herself. No harm had been done; Danby and all of the horses were safe. Nothing had happened. That cross would be too hard to bear. Lilian gave further thought to what Barney had said. "It does seem rather strange, Barney. I thought that one was too heavy to lift. I have never seen them moved. Grandpapa had it made just for the stable."

"No, m'lady. We can lift them, but I 'ave never had an occasion to do so."

"Would you please push my chair to the house? I think it might be difficult to push it myself back up the slope." She offered a weak smile. "I fear my arm muscles have slackened while in London."

"Yes, of course, m'lady." Barney took the brake off and pushed Lilian and Cooper to the rear portico, where Winston was already waiting. Barney gave a polite nod and headed back towards the stable.

The door slowly swung closed behind them as Winston rolled her toward the dining room, where she then joined her family.

~

No one noticed the dark-haired, moustached man, garbed in black, step from behind the shrubs. He put a pencil in his pocket and stared at the door for a moment before turning to leave.

CHAPTER 12

Harlow was glad he had not been alone on this journey to Cornwall. It was nice to have Max with him. Nearly four days on horseback reminded him of the vastness of his country. Luckily, his valet, Haydon, had ridden ahead and reserved accommodations at all the inns en route. Having rooms secured was a tremendous boon. With the Season ending, many families were returning to their country estates for a respite from the haze of London. He estimated they had fewer than five miles still to cover and should be there by ten of the clock despite these last miles being some of the hardest.

"It is fortuitous that we have seen no signs of highwaymen during this ride. With many of the titled heading to their country homes, that has been a pleasant surprise," he remarked to Max.

"Very." Max's response sounded automatic. He glanced at his friend, assuring himself Max had not nodded off. "Max, Tintagel is but a few miles ahead. I propose we rest for a few hours when we arrive and then go out to the lookout site." Max shot him a look of surprise that confirmed his friend's mind had been elsewhere. "A penny for your thoughts," he coaxed.

"I was thinking about Maggie. Her birthday will be in three weeks. I am hoping to be there to celebrate it with her." Max patted his pocket. "I have a present for her."

"I know you miss Maggie and baby Nathan. Did you buy jewellery?" he enquired. "A ring, perhaps?" He sounded inquisitive and was chafed by his own questions. The look of testiness on his friend's face encouraged him to clarify his thoughts. "Considering our commission, I would ask if that was wise to bring on the road?" Max narrowed his eyes, and Harlow immediately regretted his admonishing tone. "I apologize. Forget what I said. No one would dare challenge you for your baubles, my friend."

Max gave a dismissive shrug of the shoulders.

Without doubt, the gift would be jewellery. The man was besotted. A twinge of jealousy coursed through Harlow when he realized he had no birthdays, apart from his mother's, to fret over.

"You are wrong with what you are thinking—on both counts," Max interrupted Harlow's self-pity. "This is not jewellery, and I do not want to misplace it. It has happened before, so I am being careful with this gift."

"*Now* you have my attention. What could be small enough to have in your pocket, yet not a trinket?"

"I penned her a poem, if you must know. It is simple enough. She challenged me to write one last year, and I have not done so until now. I plan to surprise her. Maggie has every jewel she could want." Max gave Harlow a bemused smile and stared off into the distance. "The sun is peering through the clouds. It looks as if it will be a glorious day. It has been a lucky circumstance that the rain has come only at night these past days. Willow hates travelling in the rain, and I agree with her."

"*Wait!* You wrote your wife a *poem?*" Harlow asked, unable to hide his amusement. "Let me guess! Roses are red, violets are blue, you are my honey and I love you!" he remarked, pleased at his quip.

"I would never have thought you a romantic, but that is good, Harlow. You have turned into Lord Byron before my eyes," Max replied, his voice mocking. "Luckily, I need not copy that poem. I have created my own."

"I wait to hear this with bated breath." Harlow laughed as he spoke.

"Very well. I can share." Max slid out the message, unfolded it and held it out in front of him. "I want you to know it is only because you are like a brother to me that I feel like sharing this. I swear, if you scoff at me..."

"Get on with it," Harlow cut in, smiling. The two men slowed their horses to a trot.

Max drew a deep breath and exhaled slowly. "Keep in mind, Harlow, I have never done this before..."

'Twas a night like the one when we first met,
I can, for my life, I will never forget.
Bright stars in the sky, they twinkled above,
When we danced and kissed, and our hearts found love.
They sent you from my life,
My future, my love, it was spurned,
My lips and my heart,
Oh, the misery, it burned.
Until the day that I found you,
When our wounds were so deep,
I fought to ignore you,
The price—my heart, was too steep.
Stars and moonlight lit up the sky,
I found you, broken of body,
A small dog by your side.

A stalwart defender he was,
My admiration it grew,
Two hearts led the way, we finally knew,
My life, my love,
Maggie, so true, forever my bride.

Harlow remained silent for a long moment. "Your wife will love it, Max."

"Thank you. Nonetheless, I had better still come home with a trinket for her," he joked. "She will expect that." He folded the paper and placed the poem in his pocket. "I can deny her nothing."

"Your poem tells your story. Maggie disappeared with nary a word and broke your heart. You found her when she needed a hero," Harlow added, hoping he sounded consoling.

Max smiled. The two men urged their mounts to go a little faster, but stayed at a reasonable pace, allowing conversation.

"It has been nearly a year," Harlow remarked, "yet it still baffles the mind that you found each other again." He gave a hollow laugh. "I cannot mock your poem. I wish I had someone who would beg me for one." His throat squeezed. He wanted to wish for love, but fear of scaring a ladylove stayed his heart.

"I believe that anything is possible, Harlow," Max whispered. "I think being leg-shackled to the right person could help heal your soul. It would seem your heart has already decided, so your mind may have to become accustomed to the notion."

"I am still not certain. My nightmares have increased." Harlow tried to keep his tone light. Inside, he wondered if Max could be right. "Marriage had not entered my mind until you showed me that bet at White's."

"You are saying the bet was a good thing?" Max nudged, taunting.

"I would not go quite as far as that. I will draw someone's cork if I find out who owns that bet," Harlow replied.

"You would hit the widow? Are your feathers that ruffled?" Max arched a brow, giving a cynical laugh.

"No, of course I would not. When I find the man who wrote it, however, he will be in the suds." He urged his horse forward. A large flock of geese suddenly flew from the thick woodland beside them. Max's talent had fogged his senses. "We were not paying attention, and I fear we are being followed."

"The birds?" Max whispered.

"Only a large animal or person would create such a hasty exodus from the trees. Look, there are hundreds of them. Let us ride, and swiftly. There is a fork under a mile yonder which circles to the left and then back to rejoin the road. I would rather see who is following us."

Thick copses of trees hugged the road on each side. It was the perfect place for highwaymen. Of all things, they did not need that distraction. Harlow silently chided himself for not paying attention and becoming preoccupied with his troubles. *I should be more knowing than that,* he thought. Fortunately, the way ahead promised more grassy pasture interspersed with smaller stands of trees.

"The fork lies beyond the next bend." He pointed and mouthed the words.

Max nodded, and they urged their horses on at a clip. The fork was half a mile, just before Tintagel. They took it, riding across a field of high grasses, keeping dust to a minimum until they spied another large stretch of thick woodland they could use for cover.

They had barely hidden when a rider in black spurred down the road in front of them, riding a dapple-grey horse.

He appeared to be in a hurry; the horse's neck was outstretched, and foam dripped from its mouth. The rider held his head low, covered by a wide-brimmed black hat. The only feature Harlow was able to see was a thin, distinctive moustache, and yet he felt sure there was something familiar.

"Did you recognize him?" Harlow asked.

"No, I did not. His moustache style is rather odd for this area. They are not generally so well-manicured," Max responded. He angled his head in the rider's direction. "We should follow, I have a suspicion we will see him again."

"Agreed." Harlow urged his horse forward, and the men once again set off at a fast pace, following the dust kicked up by the grey all the way into Tintagel.

"I see nothing of the rider," Harlow said as they drew rein outside an inn made of light-coloured stone and dark wood. "However, this is where we are staying. Haydon booked rooms for us here at *The Merry Maiden*. We should get some rest. De...Cressey is supposed to leave word of where to meet him. I believe it will be an encrypted message or similar." They urged their horses towards the stable, beside the inn. A tall, thin young man with blond hair walked towards them.

"Can I take yer horses, m'lords?" he offered. The two men dismounted and handed the reins to the ostler before unhooking their bags from their saddles. "I be Michael, the head ostler," he continued. "Do you need the shoes checked? Smithy be over there." He pointed to the blacksmith's shop where a burly, bald-headed man hammered iron on the anvil with heavy thuds.

"Thanking you," Harlow responded. "Yes, have the smith look them over, if you will. Feed and water them as well. We may require them in a few hours, so they need to be well rested. Oh, and give them a rub down too, please."

"Yes, m'lords." He stood there, waiting.

"Here you go," Harlow added, realizing that the boy was waiting for coin. He gave him a shilling. "Take good care of them."

"I will do that, m'lords." Michael tugged the brim of his hat. Pocketing the largesse, he walked the two horses into the stable.

"I hope Haydon booked two rooms. He set off shortly after DeLacey left to join his family, so he should have had time. If not, he was to leave me a note here, with instructions on where he secured lodgings instead," Harlow commented as they walked towards the rear entrance of the inn.

Max nudged him. "Do not turn around until we reach the door, but the grey horse we just chased is tied at the tavern across the street."

Harlow peripherally peered across the street as they opened the door to the inn and gave a brief nod of acknowledgement to Max. They entered the inn and stood for a moment allowing their eyes to adjust to the dim light. Dark panelling covered the walls. Small-paned windows obscured by red curtains, allowed only partial light to enter. The smell of cheap tallow and ale greeted them.

"Welcome to *The Merry Maiden,* m'lords!" A lanky, bespectacled innkeeper greeted them. His head was mostly bald except for a shock of white-blond hair that was combed over the front of his head. "'Ow can 'Oi assist ye this fine afternoon?"

"Lord Harlow and Lord Worsley, landlord. I believe you have rooms in our names?" The innkeeper stepped behind the waist-high desk behind him and opened a ledger. He leaned low into the page, squinting to see the entries, travelling down the page with the tip of his finger.

"Ah! Here it is. Me misses is upstairs cleaning 'er rooms. She will be down directly. Your man said ye would be here by this evening."

"Thank you. Have you a private parlour? We would appreciate a meal if you have anything suitable for two hungry travellers?" Max queried.

"Yes, we do, sirs. Please to follow me. There is a lady using it. She is eating alone, but there are two large tables and ye can 'ave yer own. Will that be acceptable to ye?" the innkeeper inquired.

"As long as she can tolerate our dusty appearance, we have no objection. Bring a pitcher of ale and two glasses, will you?" Harlow added. "What are you serving today?"

"'Tis our day for stargazy pie; if ye like pilchards, ye will find this tasty. We also have fresh Cornish pasty and clam soup."

Harlow glanced at Max, who shrugged. "We will take the stargazy pie, and the Cornish pasty, and a platter of your yarg cheese and crackers." He had discovered the yarg cheese on their last visit and enjoyed its light, creamy, cheddar taste.

The innkeeper bobbed his head in deference and pointed to the door next to him. "I will let ye know when yer rooms are ready."

The two men entered the room. Harlow saw a flash of red satin, blonde hair and a black hat feather as another door across the room closed. They looked at one another. Although behind him, Max had seen the disappearing figure too. His eyebrows rose. Harlow scrambled across the room, banging into the chairs as he reached the door to look. Another door to the outside closed, and he ran quickly to open it. There was no sign of the woman.

"Damnation, I see nothing." He stared at Max, puzzled. "I was certain that was her. Perhaps I am placing more significance on these events than there can possibly be." He closed the door, shaking his head. However, he could not ignore the chill that crossed his shoulders.

"I know what you will say, Harlow. I thought that. Our

horses may be being shod. If she is here, we will find out why later." Max spoke slowly, "We do not want to draw undue attention to ourselves by haring through the streets."

"It seems too coincidental. I cannot shake the menacing feeling her presence just gave me. I am convinced that was her..." Harlow shook his head, trying to clear it. "You are right, as usual. We need to eat and rest. She cannot have seen us, which makes me believe the widow knows we are here but is unaware we have spotted her."

"*If* that was indeed her." Max corrected.

"As you will. We both saw the same, did we not? We know that figure was she. The thing we do not yet grasp is why the widow is here. DeLacey will meet with us soon. He may have more information. I believe we should discuss this further in our room after we eat." Harlow dropped his voice to a low murmur. Fatigue was catching up with him.

He pulled out a chair and sat down. Max followed. The door opened and what looked to be the innkeeper's wife walked in with a maid behind her, both carrying trays. The maid looked to be an older child and stayed close to the woman.

"M'girl, Lizzy, will serve ye yer ale, while I set your dinner, good sirs. Yer room is ready. Cleaned it meself. Yer things 'ave been taken upstairs. Your chambers be the third and fourth doors on the right. My, trade 'as been brisk today," she added, smiling. "We 'ave a small party in this day and are a bit behindhand. My apologies fer any inconvenience. The rooms all latch from the inside." The short, pudgy woman helped Lizzy set the table.

"The food looks very good. Thank you." Harlow picked up his glass and sipped. The ale was cool and frothy and tasted good on his parched throat. "'Tis good." He inclined his head in appreciation.

Both women bobbed a curtsey and left the room.

"I have never had stargazy pie," Max said after the door closed, "but I'm game to try it."

"It is a local specialty. I find it tasty, but the fish heads eyeing me thus, do not appeal. I have to close my eyes and eat."

Max gave a hearty laugh, causing Harlow also to chuckle. They clinked glasses and dug into their repast.

An hour later they made their way to their rooms, stopping first at Harlow's. They found a note on the small table next to the bed, sealed with a wax letter 'C', addressed to Harlow.

Saw you arrive. Meet me at the previously discussed location at seven of the clock. C.

Harlow passed the note to Max.

"Good. Maybe he can shed some light on the widow's movements. I hope everything can wait until I have at least two hours' rest," Max muttered.

"The long ride and a full belly makes me crave sleep." Harlow nodded agreement. "We have several hours before we need to be there. A nap beckons." He looked out of the window at the quiet street. "The post office is probably less than half an hour away."

Max nodded and stopped at the door. "I think we should meet with Avalon soon."

Visions of Lilian flew across Harlow's mind. "I agree. I would like to make sure they have arrived safely at home. I sent him a note through Haydon and indicated we would visit today if possible." *What I really want is to see Lilian.*

CHAPTER 13

Lilian sat up and stretching, looked around. She felt refreshed. Nevertheless, it took a moment to get her bearings and realize that she was no longer in that dusty, bumpy coach, or waking up at a coaching inn. Her bedchamber at Elysium Manor was a welcome sight. She adored the Chinese cane furniture her grandmama had given her—a small writing desk, medallion back cane chair and a matching canopy bed. The furniture added to the elegance of the room with its gold on white wood and fabric of sky blue with large ivory and gold flowers. "Waking up in this room always makes me feel cheerful," she muttered to herself. Determined not to waste a second of the day , she rang for her maid. The sun was shining and a soft breeze from her open window, carrying the smell of roses, stirred her senses. She looked over at Cooper, softly snoring on the pillow next to her.

"Wake up, little fellow!" She nudged him gently, and he stood up and stretched. "That is a funny way to stretch, but I will wager it makes your back feel good. I wish I could stretch in that way." She loved learning his personality. It had been almost a week, and he had become very comfortable. His neck was almost completely healed, too.

Her foot itched, and she absently threw back the cover and scratched it. The door to her room opened, and Clara walked in, carrying a tray of food. Lilian pulled the cover back.

"Good morning, Clara." She could not prevent her voice from bubbling with happiness.

"Good morning, m'lady. Ye seem in fine spirits today! I 'ave brought ye breakfast. 'Er ladyship wishes to go to town. She plans to leave in two hours and asked me to make ye and Lady Lydia ready. She wishes ye both to go with her. I let ye sleep as long as I dared—and may I say as how it pleases me it did ye some good," she said jovially.

Clara set the tray she was carrying on a table. "I 'as brought yer fav'rites—coddled eggs, bacon, buttered toast and a few slices of ham. A good meal is needful to start the day!" Her maid walked to the window and pushed the blue curtains apart, tying them open at the sides.

"It smells delicious." Lilian sat up. "I would love to go with Mama to town. It will be pleasant to visit the shops. I would like some ribbons and other fripperies to refresh my wardrobe and..." Lilian stopped talking when she realized that her mood was lighter than it had been in months. *What has accounted for that?* She glanced at her puppy. Cooper sat quietly on the floor, looking up at the tray. "As beggars go, you are very polite, are you not?" she quipped, amused at this aspect of his personality.

Clara uncovered a small white bowl at the back of the tray. "This is fer Cooper. Yer mother suggested I bring his breakfast up here, too." She cackled. "I have not seen yer Mama take such interest in an animal in an age." When Lilian raised her brows at this over-familiarity, Clara added lightly, "'Tis nice to see. She has even instructed Cook on a suitable diet for him." Sounding more like a goose than ever, she set the bowl down and stepped back.

Cooper edged over, sniffing cautiously. He gave a quick look of appreciation and dived into his breakfast, nearly inhaling the bowl of food.

"Was that a smile? Clara, I am convinced he smiled!" Lilian exclaimed. "My dear little friend is just the tonic for me. He lightens my heart."

"I think he does, but so does Lord Harlow," Clara added softly, and her face coloured immediately. "Begging your pardon, m'lady."

Instead of being upset by Clara's remark, Lilian found herself comforted. John had shared a piece of himself with her; he had trusted her. His nightmares must be terrible to keep such a happy man from sharing his life with someone. A twinge of protectiveness coursed through her. *I want to be that person.*

Clara laid Lilian's lavender and white satin day gown on her chair and placed freshly laundered undergarments on top.

"Finish breaking yer fast, m'lady, and I will be back in a jiffy to get ye dressed." She patted Lilian's hand and left the room.

Lilian loved Clara's choice of gown. It was her favourite, mostly because of its small lavender and white floral print. Her father never failed to compliment her when she wore it, saying the dress made her eyes look *turquoise*. She knew from the many comments received over her lifetime that her eyes were an uncommon colour. Distractedly, she moved the tray onto her lap, and suddenly realized how hungry she was. Cooper would not be the only one to attack food this morning, she reflected as she chewed a piece of ham.

Dressed, with time to spare, she rang for Winston and asked

him to help her sit on her blue velvet window seat, so she could read A Lady's newest novel, *Mansfield Park.* She often wondered who wrote behind the pseudo name, A Lady, but felt fortunate to have acquired a copy in London, as most of the bookshops had already sold out. Reaching over to Cooper, who had curled up next to her, she softly scratched him behind the ears.

"Lady Bertram of Mansfield Park confines her little pugs to her lap. We shall not do that to you, my sweet boy. Perhaps this afternoon we may visit Danby again. I will take more apples." His ears perked up at her voice and he wriggled closer.

Hearing footsteps in the hall, she placed her book down in the corner. "I believe it is time to leave for town, Cooper. You will need to behave while I am gone." She playfully touched his nose. "Do not eat too much. I fear Cook is developing an affection for you as well, and that could lead to difficulty if you grow too portly!" The small dog whimpered, and jumped down from the seat, as if protesting her admonishment about Cook. The timing of his whimper amused Lilian. "There now, I did not say she would not feed you at all!"

The door opened and Clara came in, followed by Winston. "Are ye ready to go downstairs, m'lady?" She hated this exercise because of all it represented but was glad to have a wheel-chair upstairs and downstairs. It gave her a small amount of independence to move about the house on her own.

When Lilian nodded, Winston picked her up from the window seat. Cooper gave a short, protective bark and followed them to the stairs.

"I declare! I believe he's looking after ye, m'lady. 'E clearly sees ye as 'is and his alone," Clara commented in her usual lively tone, as she made her way behind Winston downstairs.

Cooper followed closely behind Winston, which had quickly become his custom.

"Ah, excellent, my dear! I was just about to ring for you, Winston." The Countess stepped back. "Lady Lydia is awaiting her sister in the carriage."

The burly footman nodded, and carried Lilian to the shiny dark grey coach, placing her onto the dark blue velvet seat. It was her mother's favourite coach, perhaps because of the greys that drew it. *At least it is not the conveyance we arrived home in yesterday. They are probably still cleaning it,* Lilian mused as she adjusted her dress. I am sure they will need to correct a permanent dip in the seat from my sitting there so long! She peered around the curtain and saw her mother hurrying down the steps, carrying Lilian's bonnet and the pelisse draped over her arm. *There must be a bee in Mama's bonnet,* she thought wryly. Her mother did not dally when she decided upon something, but this excursion felt rather rushed. The weather was still warm enough that it felt better to travel without her coat. She had planned to place it on just before they arrived.

"You look in high ropes today, sister," Lydia spoke up from across the carriage.

"I do feel more rested," Lilian replied.

"It seems a little more than that," Lydia added in a droll tone.

"Really, that is all," Lilian protested, keeping her voice light. She was unwilling to allow Lydia to draw her into a discussion about Lord Harlow, especially with Mama present. *What if he has changed his mind about giving us opportunity to develop a connection? I would never hear the end of the subject.*

"I did not mean to upset you yesterday, Lilian," Lydia intoned, eyeing their mother. The Countess was giving last-minute instructions to Clara in front of the steps leading to the house.

"Beg pardon, I… Oh, do you mean giving me that cane? It is beautiful. I will try, but I do not want to disappoint everyone. I have no feeling in my legs. I am afraid to stand and fall."

"I am convinced that will not happen. I would like to help you try, if you will let me." Lydia moved the curtain on her side of the carriage. "Mama is coming. We will discuss it later."

The Countess entered the conveyance and sat down next to Lydia.

Mama prefers having her back to the driver, Lilian thought, then shook her head, dismissing the notion.

"Mama, do you think the *Confectionery Shop* still serves ices?" Lilian asked. "I should love one if we have the time. She remembered John's comment in the park about raspberry ices and wondered if that was his favourite flavour.

"That would be nice; it might also be a pleasing way to complete our excursion. I hope you girls do not mind being hurried along. Your father suggested this trip to town, thinking it would do us all good, and I should like to take the opportunity to order us all a new gown each. I was thinking a deep lavender for you, Lydia, and for you, Lilian, perhaps a cyan blue or even magenta silk," she proclaimed. "However, the colours will be your choices."

"That sounds lovely, Mama," Lydia piped up. "Lord Yarstone said he would pay a visit shortly. I have not been so forward as to offer, of course, but do you think he might be able to stay here instead of taking rooms at an inn?"

"I daresay that could be arranged, my dear. We all enjoy Lord Yarstone's company," her mother responded.

Any minute now, she will turn to me. Lilian glanced at her sister and noticed her hoydenish smirk. *Kicking up larks, are you? I will delight in repaying you, little sister,* Lilian promised, giving Lydia a sardonic smile when their mother was looking the other way.

"Lilian, your father made mention of the fact that Lord Harlow plans to visit Tintagel. We must not be behindhand with our hospitality. I should be happy to offer him accommodations also," her mother added.

Lilian pretended astonishment. "Thank you, Mama. That is most kind, I am sure. However, although Lord Harlow informed me that he and Lord Worsley had business in Cornwall. he made no declaration of a specific visit, as Lord Yarstone has done." Gently, she skirted around the topic.

"How odd. Perhaps he meant it as a surprise," her mother added gaily. "For indeed, your father received a missive today, from Lord Harlow, asking if he could receive both he and Lord Worsley later this afternoon." Lady Avalon fiddled with her gold-coloured pelisse and gave a slight tilt to her bonnet.

Without conscious thought, Lilian's mouth formed an *O*. *What could he be about, meeting with Father?* She knew he was not ready to offer for her. A light quiver shook her as she felt a sense of apprehension.

The smell of sea salt and the sound of sheep baaing softly in the background meant they were approaching the village. As the carriage advanced into the town of Tintagel, the earth road soon changed to cobblestone, making the ride somewhat bumpier. Thatched roofs and slate ones adorned the tops of small white limestone and dark timber buildings, lined up in rows branching from the main road. The sight cheered her, and she refused to think anything dreadful could be about to happen. Mama's voice cut into her musings.

"My darlings, I think two hours in town should be sufficient, do you not agree?"

I should have known something was amiss when Mama insisted on leaving so early. She was obviously up to her old tricks, hoping we are home in time to entertain Lord Harlow. Lilian was aware of a certain irritation but found it difficult to maintain. Her mother's dream for her had become her own dream, but she would never admit to it. She could not take disappointment.

Her mother tapped the top of the carriage and it stopped in front of Madame Chandos' shop. Their friendship had spanned the two ladies' lifetime, and Mama always commissioned several dresses when they returned from London. Madame Chandos' seamstresses turned out very elegant work, at a fraction of the price to be found in London. Mama could spend hours poring over patterns and fabrics, especially if a new shipment of lace had arrived.

Winston assisted Lilian into her wheel-chair, and then pushed her into the shop. Most of the shop's light came from the large glass window at the front and two oil lamps at the rear, behind a long counter. Fabrics and laces covered large, flat, waist-high tables. Shelves lined the walls with hundreds of bolts of fabric standing side by side, arranged according to colour and texture. High tables flanked the counter on each side with tall stools, giving space for the patrons to examine large pattern books. The back wall opened to two small dressing rooms for the clients and a tiny office. Lilian looked around her, secretly hoping that Mama's sense of urgency would aid them in leaving here quickly. The shop door tinkled when they entered, alerting the modiste to their presence, and she hurried to welcome them.

"*Bienvenu, chères amies,*" the shop owner gushed. "It is my pleasure to see you, my friend. How may I assist you?"

"Madame, it has been an age. We arrived home only yesterday, and I wanted to make this my first call."

"I am so glad to see all of you, my lady. Did you have a

good stay in London? I had planned to visit, but I have been very busy of late," the modiste replied.

"My daughters and I need new morning and evening dresses. Perhaps two each. I have some colours in mind, but of course, the final selection will be theirs—unless their usual good taste deserts them." A fabric near the corner of the table caught their mother's eye, and she walked over to it.

"Your girls are so beautiful," the proprietress flattered. "Lady Lydia adores the pinks, but perhaps a gown of cream and lavender would be pretty."

"That is just what I had imagined," oozed Mama. She turned to Lydia, who was fingering some lace.

"Ah, you have good taste, Lady Lydia. That has only just arrived. It is my latest shipment of Belgium lace; the finest from Brussels," Madame Chandos added proudly. "It would make a beautiful overdress with this lovely lavender satin." She held the fabrics together, the sheen catching the light from the window.

Lydia nodded her approval. "That would be lovely, Mama." She had spotted a magenta velvet off to one side and directed their mother's attention to it. "Might I have a new riding habit, Mama? This is beautiful."

Mama put her finger to her lips. "I had a similar colour in mind for your sister, but if you have set your heart on it, and if Lilian has no objection, I see no reason to refuse. It would be most charming on you."

All eyes turned towards Lilian. "I am happy with whatever you decide, Mama, truly."

"Ah, *chèrie*, you will be happy. Wait and see." Madame Chandos shepherded her mother and sister to view the pattern books.

Lilian did not feel any real need to choose. Her mother and Lydia knew her taste, and it was uncomfortable with the wheel-chair. Instead, she moved over to the counter where the ribbons and other fripperies were arranged, just as the door tinkled open. A blonde woman entered, wearing a yellow and black striped satin gown and a matching black hat with large black feathers. She turned, and Lilian recognized her immediately as Lady Poinz. *What was the widow Poinz doing here?* Lilian had never noticed her before the ball in London earlier in the month—but then, the woman had only come to her attention because of her flirtatious behaviour towards Lord Harlow. A cold tremor ran over her body.

"Good day." The woman stepped in her direction.

At that moment, Madame Chandos hurried to the front of the shop. "Lady Poinz, may I be of assistance?" she asked nervously.

Mama and Lydia walked up from behind. "Madame, I believe that you have an understanding of our requirements. I shall await your pleasure in due course. We must away; I am expecting guests."

Lady Poinz looked first towards Mama and then at Lilian. "There is no need to hurry away on my account, but if I might ask a tiny favour?" Pausing briefly, she continued, "Lady Lilian, when you next see Lord Harlow, please be sure to give him my sincerest regards." A smile flickered on her lips.

Her mother drew herself up and stepped closer to Lilian, meeting Lady Poinz's stare. "I am sure you can drop him a note, should you have a message to deliver, Catherine," she said in hushed tones. Her eyes flashed with anger.

A moment of silence ensued as the women appeared to take measure of each other.

"Countess, I do not care for your tone," the woman hissed.

"Indeed? Your sensibilities mean nothing to me. I do not care for your bonnet," her mother said icily. Pointedly, she turned to her friend. “If you will excuse us, Madame Chandos? Thank you for your time and I will look for your best attentions, as usual. You will send word when the gowns are complete?”

“Yes, your ladyship, the moment they are ready.”

CHAPTER 14

A bright afternoon sun woke him. Glancing outside at the position of the golden orb, Harlow judged he had slept for several hours. He pulled out his pocket watch, hoping he had not overslept. Three hours had passed; while it was more than he had expected, they had both been bone weary. The nap had done him good. Once dressed, he walked next door and tapped on Max's door.

"'Tis open, Harlow."

Harlow pushed open the door to find Max pulling on his boots. "Do you allow anyone to enter?" He scoffed playfully at his friend.

"I knew it was you. I heard you stamping into your boots and knew you had finished dressing. I presumed you would be here to check on me." Max covered his bed with the sheet and blanket provided and plumped up his pillows. Without turning, he spoke, "Military training, in case you are thinking of chiding me. It is nice to go to sleep in a bed that looks like no one has slept in it before you."

"I want to laugh, I swear I do," Harlow answered, "despite the fact I do the same thing." He stared at the bed. "I wish that had been the only habit I had kept from the army," he added bleakly.

They found Michael mucking out a stall. The young man set his pitchfork against the wall and helped saddle the horses.

"Good day to you, m'lords. Yon smith replaced two of the shoes on this one." He pointed to Max's horse, Willow. "He replaced the left hind on this one." He patted Harlow's horse on the rump. "I've fed 'em both some sweet hay and oats and brushed 'em well."

"Thank you." Harlow tossed him two silver shillings. "Give one to the smith for his work and keep the other for yourself."

"Thank ye kindly, m'lord!" The young man fingered the shillings in his hands and immediately secured them in his pocket.

Harlow mounted his mare. "One more thing."

"M'lord?" The ostler looked up.

"I hesitate to ask…have you seen a lady in a red dress? We thought we recognized a friend earlier, a lady who was partaking of luncheon when we arrived. Unfortunately, we just missed her. She left through the side door as we were entering the dining room."

Michael's eyes shifted nervously, and he cast a sidelong glance. Satisfied they were not being observed, he edged closer.

"M'lords, pardon me impudence, I know that one ain't no friend of yourn. She comes 'ere often—stays at the tavern across the way. She is a mean one." He paused, still watchful. "And 'ave a care, the walls about 'ere 'ave ears." The young man grimaced and lightly tipped his brown felt hat. He cast about the yard once again before walking to the stable door and collecting his pitchfork.

"That was odd," Harlow reflected aloud as soon as they had passed the first few buildings.

"It certainly was," Max replied.

"The post office should be about a quarter of a mile down this road, on the right. DeLacey may be there already." Harlow muttered.

Max took a big sniff of the air and spoke up loudly as a farmer in a cart approached from around a bend.

"I like the smell of the coast. My parents were given to taking the family in both warm and cold weather. Mother is convinced that there are healing properties to be had from swimming in the ocean," Max observed. When the farmer had passed, he turned to Harlow. "My apologies. It was the only thing I could think of when I saw the farmer and wanted to make sure you noticed the white horse," he said as he gestured with his head to emphasize the horse now behind him.

"Your sudden excursion into the realms of memory stirred me from my reverie. Thank you," he responded sarcastically. "Since you bring up the topic, are you familiar with the contraptions employed by women to swim in the ocean?" He shook his head in disbelief. "Men can strip down and at once immerse themselves in the waves. Women, however, wear enough clothing to sink a small vessel. To be required to be pulled out to sea in a bathhouse on wheels seems over done," Harlow added. "Has your mother ever tried that?" he asked.

"Good God, Harlow, this is no time for such notions. "I do not even want to *think* of my mother in a bathing-machine, rolling into the sea. Besides, it is doubtful we will see anything like that off the Cornish coast. The ocean floor is too rocky," Max retorted.

"Are you saying you wish they could *remove all their clothing* and jump straight in the water?" Harlow persisted, full of mirth. "That would certainly have a few healing properties for me. What say you?"

"Enough. I wish I had not said anything. Keep your mind on our task," Max countered. They turned off the road onto the gravelled one before the building that shared the post office and the local draper's shop. "It looks abandoned. I imagined people would be here," he added as they dismounted and walked their horses towards the back of the property.

"Today is Saturday. I do not believe it is open every day. However, I cannot agree no one is here. It is a walkable distance. Anyone could arrive."

They tied their horses in the shade of a large oak tree and waited. When they were involved in a commission such as this, they watched the opposite sides of the property. Max tapped his friend when he spotted DeLacey step from behind a massive mulberry bush, leading his horse behind him.

"A praiseworthy entrance," Harlow remarked. "I had not considered hiding in a mulberry bush until now. They make excellent cover." He strode over and pulled off a twig of black fruit. Mulberry bushes and other shrubs made up a garden area that appeared long since abandoned. "An excellent resource," he said, popping one of the mulberries into this mouth.

"I rather like them myself," DeLacey retorted wryly. He looked around and motioned them together. "I think we discussed the farmer's signal, did we not?"

"The white horse and the farmer we spoke of with Cressey in Town?" Harlow tested, making sure they were the same. "I think we met him just now as we rode through town."

"The very one. He rode back earlier this morning, along the ridge. It fits. The Prince Regent told me he expects a large shipment of confiscated brandies and laces from France to pass through. A small payroll was also rumoured to be included on the boat. It is manned by Lieutenant Pelham, whose star is rising in the British Navy since he has been reclaiming goods for the government. His ship just took down two pirate ships while on patrol. These are goods that were confiscated.

"So, this ship sails through tomorrow night?" Harlow declared more than asked.

DeLacey nodded.

"I assume Pelham knows the importance of this operation and is in on the deceit," Max said in a questioning tone.

"You have the right of it. The free traders dream of finding a bounty of supplies such as this. The Prince Regent wants to save this ship and its cargo and intends we trap the traitor. Only two other people within the navy know the route Pelham will take—the Admiral and his secretary."

"The Rear Admiral?" Harlow put his question matter-of-factly and glanced at Max. This was not the first operation where they had suspected someone in high authority of alerting the enemy.

"I notice this surprises neither of you. The secretary, however, is unaware of the trap," DeLacey acknowledged in a low voice. "His guilt seems conclusive if the signal I described turns out to be true. If this ship is lured and attacked, we snare both the snitch and the head of this smuggling ring. *That* is the most important outcome. Alert your associate within the Dragoons and bid them be hidden, ready to attack, before nightfall," DeLacey ordered, marking off each instruction with his fingers. "You have both met my contact."

Harlow looked up, startled. The only people they had met were the ostler and the innkeeper's family, although they had also caught a glimpse of the widow.

"*Of course.* Michael," he said, inclining his head.

"Yes," DeLacey replied in a smug tone. "Tip him the nod when you need to get word to me. We can trust him. He has proven himself invaluable to me. The smugglers falsely accused his uncle of collaborating with the Revenue men and killed him. I liked the man. He was a good man and the only father Michael has known. He seeks to avenge his uncle's death.

"I see," Harlow responded. He hoped Michael's loyalty, based as it was on revenge, would prove solid. This was a perilous mission.

"Have you become familiar with the caves along the coast —the caves under the castle?

"Somewhat. We have been watching the area off and on for a year, now, using your father's property to gain access," Max responded.

"Excellent! I found a little-known cave located close to King's Cave. Large boulders and shrubs hide its narrow opening, and there are no signs of use for many a long year. I will meet you there before noon tomorrow." DeLacey dropped to his knees and sketched a drawing in the sandy loam of the yard. "This is the line of the cliffs and here is the cave I am using." He drew the shore and explained how to get to King's Cave. Pointing out the location of his cave, he drew what resembled a bend to the coast and placed an X on a rendering of a cave. "This is where we think they are operating from."

"We watched men coming and going from that cave, moving cargo," Max supplied. He glanced at Harlow.

DeLacey was silent for a moment before speaking. "The Prince Regent's orders are to get the leader and save the ship *and* its cargo. This will get dangerous. A lantern will signal the boat, and Pelham will drift close to the coast. His sloop is fast, well armoured, turns easily, and can also easily hug close to the coast. A ruthless woman leads the gang. You already suspect her."

"The widow Poinz," Harlow murmured.

"Exactly. She has free rein around here. The villagers help her because they benefit, yet they fear her. Normally, she runs the enterprise from London. According to Michael, a dark-haired, wiry man is her co-conspirator. He wears a strange, curving moustache. I have not seen him, and we have been powerless to catch the widow with her smuggling operation. Your information relating to her recent behaviour confirmed several things we suspected. Lady Poinz turned her late husband's many holdings into shielding and commerce opportunities for her operation; however, her own carelessness has led us to suspect her. The woman has no consideration for people, and she retaliates at the merest slight." DeLacey grew silent for a moment. "My sources confirm she has arrived to oversee this attack. The village supports her, as I have said. I believe they are all too frightened for their skins to do otherwise. Even the local vicar blesses their efforts in the fair trade. The six Revenue men who were killed in their cutter off the shore here, lost their lives trying to catch her. The villagers know her and provide cover, and we cannot arrest the whole town. The Prince Regent has made it known he will brand her as a traitor and hang her if we catch her, despite her peerage."

"We saw her," Harlow said flatly. His concern for Lilian advanced immeasurably, even though the widow's attraction to him made no sense. "Lady Poinz appeared, somewhat oddly, in the inn—she was fleeing from the side door as we entered the dining room."

"Perhaps she wanted you to see her." DeLacey cleared the sand, wiping all evidence away before he stood up. "You have piqued the widow's interest. Her accomplice works closely with her. Watch for anyone following you."

"We will." Harlow's feelings for Lilian created a vulnerability he could not deny.

"If that is all, we have another engagement," Max added dryly as they shook hands and turned for their horses.

"My father is expecting you. Be careful about being followed," DeLacey repeated to their backs.

"We make it our business to be aware of our surroundings," Max growled harshly.

"We appreciate your help, Cressey. Do not misjudge our abilities in this operation," Harlow said in a dangerous tone he had employed on many previous such occasions. "We will meet you at the cave tomorrow."

DeLacey solemnly acknowledged the point with a slight nod of his head.

"The blighter will be your brother-in-law one day," Max murmured when they were far enough away.

Harlow said nothing. He was unsure what to say. The two men untied their horses and rode towards Elysium Manor. When they made their way up the drive, a light brown carriage with the Yarstone crest pulled away from the door and headed towards the stables.

"Not much stands between Viscount Yarstone and Lady Lydia DeLacey," Max quipped, and both men guffawed.

"We should be more surprised *not* to see him," added Harlow. "He informed me he plans to offer for Lady Lydia. The DeLacey family left sooner than he had expected, which may have foiled his romantic proposal. While he knows nothing of our operation, he is very attentive, and it could be fortuitous that he is here."

"I sense your worry about Lady Lilian. Perhaps this visit can allay some concerns," Max said with sincerity.

"You always read me so well. Yet it continually startles me when you reveal my thoughts so succinctly," Harlow whispered, adding, "I hope you are right." They handed their horses to a waiting groom and made their way up the steps.

Chambers greeted them at the door. "Welcome, Lord Harlow; Lord Worsley. Lord Avalon is in his study. He is expecting you," the retainer offered. He received their outdoor apparel and hung the various items on the coat stand. "Please to follow me."

The door to the study opened and Cooper walked out, followed by Lilian carrying a book in her lap.

"Thank you, Father," she was saying. "I…" She stopped when she saw the two men approaching. "This is a surprise," she said. "I was just going to my room to start a new book." She motioned down at the tome.

Her puppy, perhaps jealous, jumped into her lap on top of the leather-bound object.

"Cooper, behave," she commanded. "He has not met Lord Worsley before. I have also observed some rather protective behaviours since we have been home," she explained.

Both men bowed. "It is a pleasure to see you again, Lady Lilian."

She held out her hand and Harlow feathered a kiss on the back of it as manners dictated. Warmth suddenly radiated up from his collar when he noticed her father watching them.

"Perhaps you can spare a few minutes to sit in the garden after I meet with Lord Avalon."

"I would like that. I will be in the parlour," Lilian replied. "Come along, Cooper, let us be about our business and leave the gentlemen to theirs." The dog jumped down from her lap and bounded towards the front of the house. Winston appeared out of nowhere and pushed her to the parlour.

That man certainly keeps an eye on her, Harlow thought, watching them retreat.

"Gentlemen. Please come in," Lord Avalon's voice broke into Harlow's thoughts. "I alerted my Countess this morning that you would be here, so I am not sure how much of a surprise your appearance was to my daughter," he said with a wink.

Harlow and Max took the seats in front of his desk. The Earl's ebony desk sat in the centre of the room with a large picturesque window behind him, covered with green velvet curtains. A large fireplace sat on the wall to his left. Harlow's attention was immediately drawn to the painting hanging above the mantel. It pictured the Countess, seated and playing with two toddler girls while an older boy stood beside her chair, looking on. The girls were identical, except for their eyes, which the artist had captured beautifully. Fully stocked bookcases covered both sides of the room.

"I ordered a platter of sandwiches earlier. In the meantime, would either of you care for refreshment?" He opened a small cabinet to the side of his desk and took out a decanter of brandy and three glasses.

"Yes, thank you. We ate a light meal at the inn before we left this morning," Harlow said, accepting a glass. "We need to apprise you of what we have learned," he added.

"I would appreciate being taken into your confidence. I confess there is something I need to tell you, as well. Perhaps I should start," Lord Avalon answered.

"My son, who I know you have been meeting with, made known to me that I should increase security, so I engaged a small number of guards before I left London. Two men arrived a few hours ago, while the ladies were out shopping, and are settling into an empty tenant's cottage. He waved vaguely in the direction behind him. "I have also asked Winston to keep a closer eye on Lilian and Lydia."

"We noticed Yarstone's carriage when we arrived. Is he aware of anything?" Max ventured.

"No. He is here to court my daughter Lydia. Apparently, we left town too soon for his convenience." He chuckled lightly. "We have invited him to stay. The welcome extends to the two of you. The inns can be a bit rough in these parts and we have plenty of room."

A twinge of jealousy coursed through Harlow's veins, and he struggled against it. "We appreciate the offer, sir, and will consider that. Yarstone seems to have her best interests at heart," he acknowledged.

"Yes, I believe he does," the older man murmured. "I have a new concern and the more I dismiss it, the more I find I cannot. It has consumed me today," he continued. "Earlier today my head groom mentioned a strange occurrence which happened."

Harlow's insides knotted as he leaned forward towards the Earl.

"My head groom told me a lantern fell yesterday afternoon while my girls were visiting their horses. Strangely, the lantern had been lit earlier, yet it was out when it hit the ground. The wick was not even warm. Barney checked. He had filled it with fuel not long before my daughters visited.

The lantern is very large and heavy. It provides an abundance of light in front of the stable and also serves the entrance—in fact, my father placed it on a sturdy hook many years ago, and I do not believe anyone has had occasion to move it."

Harlow looked at him with alarm. "So, it was unlit when it fell? Thank goodness it was daylight. I cannot see a lantern the size of which you describe blowing itself out." *Could there have been an intended warning of some kind in this?*

"No, and we do not light it during the day unless it is gloomy, and we need light. My groom investigated and found nothing. Barney said the whole matter made his skin crawl. The man has good instincts," the Earl responded.

"We should like to look at the area, if you do not mind,

especially considering what we have told you about the widow," Max added, concern etched on his face.

"I had been about to set out there to investigate this matter when Lilian came to see me. I did not want to alarm her, so spoke to her first. Since you are both here, perhaps we can investigate together. I am concerned. Your visit has made me realize there is more to be concerned about."

Harlow and Max leaned forward, setting their glasses down.

"My wife and daughters chanced upon Lady Catherine Poinz this morning, in town. She came into the shop where they were being served and gave my daughter a message to give to you, Lord Harlow," the Earl recounted.

Harlow's insides quaked. "I swear I cannot account for the woman's interest, yet I refuse to dismiss it lightly. What did she say?"

"She deliberately made her way to Lilian and begged her to give you her sincerest regards." Lord Avalon stared down at his hands, and then looked up, his expression pained. "My daughters are very dear to me. Have you any idea what she is about?"

Dread clutched at his heart. "I do not know why she would approach your family, except for the curious interest I described to you. We feel she is plotting something, and in fact, we discussed it with your son only a few hours ago. We would very much like to visit the stable with you, Lord Avalon."

"Do you think she could have something to do with this operation? That would make sense if she thought you were getting too close," Lord Avalon ventured.

Harlow glanced at Max. "Yes," he answered. "I would like to speak with Barney."

The three men walked down to the stables. Harlow felt apprehensive and a sudden sense of urgency—and he speculated the others felt the same, based on their rapid pace and silence.

As they approached the stables, Barney came to meet them. "My lord, might I show you something?"

"Certainly. Lead the way, Barney. I would like Lord Harlow and Lord Worsley to hear what you have to say. We were just speaking of what you told me." Lord Avalon motioned towards Max and Harlow.

"'Tis this odd-looking paper I found. I cannot make out the writing. However, there looks to be a picture of the stable." He came nearer and handed the paper to the Earl.

"It appears to be a drawing of my stable yard."

"Where did you find this?" Harlow demanded.

"M'lord, I found it right here…" Barney led the three of them to the entrance of the stable. "…near where the lantern fell."

Max walked to the building, appearing to scrutinize a spot at the entry. "Lord Avalon; Harlow?" He pointed to a faint chalk mark, almost hidden by the large trunk of the sessile oak that stood at the entrance. "It could mean nothing. Have you seen this before, Barney?"

"No, m'lord, never. It looks to be an X. I 'ave no cause to make me mark on the stable wall. I ain't never seen that afore."

Fresh concern washed over Harlow. "If you are still amenable to it, Lord Avalon, we accept your offer to stay here while we are in town." He could hear the strain in his voice. "Max, I believe we should ride to town and retrieve our belongings."

CHAPTER 15

Lilian waited patiently in the parlour, trying to read her book, while Cooper slept in his basket alongside her. She spent half of the time reading and half of the time watching the door, hoping Lord Harlow would walk in at any minute for a visit. Had anyone asked what she read, she could not have related a word. Her mind had been elsewhere. Not a soul had come through the door for the hour she had been there.

Mother was lying down in her room with a headache, upset over the episode this morning. Despite being quizzed by Lydia, she had refused to enlighten them as to the obvious history between herself and Lady Poinz. Lydia and Lord Yarstone had departed to take a walk about the property, chaperoned by Clara. It would most likely be a short excursion as Clara did not care for exercise and made that clear in her complaints whenever taxed. Lilian bit her lower lip to keep from smiling, envisioning Lydia's frustration with their maid.

That left Mary to sit with Lilian in the parlour, in the event Lord Harlow did call in to pay court. The young girl made no noise and was sitting darning linens from the basket that Clara had handed her before she departed.

Lilian sighed audibly.

"Yes, m'lady?" Mary set down her darning and looked up. "Would there be anything ye need?"

"No, Mary. I apologize. I sighed because I am not a very patient person."

In answer, the young maid bobbed her head and continued her darning.

My sister is probably walking with Lord Yarstone among the apple trees. I should love to go there with John, she thought dreamily. *Except, of course, I cannot move from this dreadful wheel-chair. There are no paths I can traverse with this awkward, cumbersome machine. 'Tis neither accommodating nor romantic.* A sardonic laugh escaped her. Frustrated, she placed her book in her lap and wheeled closer to the window. A smallish man wearing a black hat stood in the shadow of the trees, staring toward her home. Alarmed, she wheeled backwards several feet.

"Mary, come here, please."

"Yes, m'lady." The young woman placed her basket down and moved to stand next to Lilian.

"Peer out of the front window and tell me if you see a man dressed in black, standing at the edge of the lake," she instructed.

The maid leaned into the window space, searching. "No, m'lady. There be no one there."

"No? You do not see him? Truly?" Her words were more a sign of exasperation than questions. Lilian wheeled her chair closer and looked again. Mary was right. The man was gone. "Thank you, Mary." She swallowed. "Perhaps the afternoon sun was playing tricks on me." She stared in the direction she had seen the figure and saw no one. How had she imagined that? She was not wont to see things that did not exist.

Maybe she should do as Mama suggested and read fewer Gothic novels.

Not convinced, Lilian redoubled her efforts, squinting to spot anything that looked like the stranger she would have sworn was there moments ago. She could see only part of the lake and the beginnings of the orchards. Most likely, her sister and Lord Yarstone were further from the house, so no one could spy on them. Lydia knew, as Lilian did herself, that there was a good chance Clara would nod off after outside exertion. She had been known to do so on occasion, especially after walking.

Grandmama had created a lovely reflection area amid the apple trees. On sunny days, the sun could strike the pond at just the right angle, making it sparkle. Two white, iron benches, framed by a small circle of lilac bushes, gave ample seating room. The bushes were often fragrant after the apple blooms had become fruit. Lilian and her sister would frequently sit there, with their horses tied up behind them, to read and watch the swans on the lake. More times than she could count, her governess had taken them there with their easels and paints.

Lydia and Lord Yarstone are probably there. Lilian was happy for her sister and hated the silly jealousy which stabbed at her heart. Lydia, more than anyone, believed she would walk again. Lilian did not even believe that. She had resigned herself to spinsterhood and a wheel-chair—until John. Now she wanted more. She wanted him.

Her father entered the room, and she looked away from the window.

"Lilian, I am afraid Lord Harlow had to leave suddenly."

Lilian felt her face crumple in disappointment, and she twisted her hands in the folds of her skirt.

"Be of good cheer, daughter. Lord Harlow has accepted my invitation to stay here." The Earl sat on the settee next to her chair and gave her hand an affectionate squeeze. "He and Lord Worsley rode back to the village to gather their possessions from the inn."

Her mood lifted immediately, and she bit back an exclamation of delight.

Her father gave her a knowing look. "They should return before dark; they plan to join us for dinner. I will apprise your mother. I need to see how she goes on, anyway." He stood up again.

Mother will be pleased. I am pleased, too.

Her father had barely left the room when she heard the sound of galloping horses. She glanced out of the window just in time to see two gentlemen disappear down the drive from the house. While she could not see them clearly, she assumed they were Lord Harlow and his associate.

"In that case, perhaps I shall retire to my room for an afternoon nap."

"I will send Winston to assist you."

"Father, *wait*!" She was unsure whether she should reveal what she had seen, or not. "Father, I looked out at the lake a few minutes past and saw a man staring at the house."

Showing evident signs of alarm, he sat down heavily. "What did he look like, Lilian?"

"I asked Mary to look, and she saw nothing, so I am not sure Mama would not be correct in telling me I have read too many Gothic romances." Involuntarily, she shuddered. "He was standing on the edge of the trees, staring up at the window. All I noticed was that he wore black. I could not see his face, apart from a large moustache which seemed to take up most of it. Now that I think on it, it was most odd in appearance.

"Your mother could be right, but it will not be a bad thing to have the matter looked into." He patted her hand. "I will speak with Winston. He and Mary will settle you in your room.

"Thank you, Father." The Earl leaned down and kissed her on the cheek. Still curious, she was about to ask her father why her mother had reacted towards Lady Poinz in the way she had but changed her mind.

Winston came in and assisted her to her room. Mary carried Cooper's basket, and the two of them followed.

Mary helped her from her day gown and placed a fresh gown for dinner over her chair in readiness.

"M'lady, a nap will do ye a power of good. Can I bring ye a hot cup of tea and some biscuits?"

"That would be nice, Mary. Thank you." Lilian laid her head on the pillow and closed her eyes, planning to wait for the tea.

The door had barely closed behind Mary when her sister came bounding into the room.

"Lilian, wake up!"

"I am not asleep, Lydia." Cooper barked and leaped up on the bed as she sat up.

"Richard plans to ask Father for my hand. He let it slip on our walk. Please be happy for me," her sister pleaded gently.

"Of course!" she said, her eyes moist with tears. "I am enormously happy for you! I am certain Father and Mama will welcome him into the family. He is perfect for you." She wiped a rogue tear from her cheek, hoping Lydia had missed it.

"You will find your prince, too, Lilian. I know it in here," Lydia said, patting at her heart."

"I want to believe you, but I cannot. Although… Father did say John—Lord Harlow—and Lord Worsley plan to stay here for a few days. Mayhap…" She wanted to have faith in her sister's words.

"I know he has feelings for you. Whenever Lord Harlow

looks your way, everyone can see it. Something seems to hold him back, but I believe he will come up to scratch soon." Sitting on the bed, Lydia held her sister tightly and whispered, "I love you, Lilian."

Lilian looked at her twin. "And I, you! It seems as though we will have a wedding to plan. That will delight our mother to no end!"

A knock on the door claimed their attention. "M'ladies. I thought you might both like some tea and biscuits." Mary set the tray down and fished into her pocket. "Little master, I've brought you a biscuit too." She held out the rusk made especially for Cooper who immediately abandoned the bed for the treat. "Do you require anything else?"

"Not at the moment, thank you, Mary," Lilian said in dismissal. The young maid bobbed a curtsy and left the room.

"You should get some rest, Lilian. This could be an exciting evening. I do not think I could close my eyes for a moment."

"I am thrilled for you, Lydia." She gave her sister a big smile.

Lydia blew a kiss and left the room, closing the door gently behind her. Lilian once more laid her head on the pillow and gave in to the hot tears which coursed down the sides of her face. Whimpering with concern, Cooper leaped back on the bed and sat close to her head, licking her tears away.

Lilian raised her head and looked towards the window. Noticing the sun had begun to set, she realized that she had slept for hours, despite thinking no respite was possible. Her sister would be engaged, and she would still be attached to a wheel-chair. A yawn on her pillow drew her attention to the small puppy that had stolen her heart. Within less than a fortnight, this little puppy had made himself at home, changed her mother into a dog enthusiast, and given her more reason to smile than she had known in a year.

She relaxed and put her head back down on her pillow, content to snuggle a few more minutes with Cooper, and remembered her father's message—its content was a huge reason to smile. With a small shriek of delight, she reached for the cord and rang for her maid.

A few minutes later, Clara walked into the bedchamber with a cup of chocolate on a small tray.

"M'lady, I was just coming to wake you. I took a nap meself. 'Twas just the thing I needed."

Lilian bit back the smile that threatened. Clara would have been rebuked, had Mama heard her remark, and perhaps she should censure her, but the old woman's declarations amused her at times.

Mary had laid out a pink floral silk and matching shoes. Clara approved of the choice and helped Lilian to dress.

"Is there a longer style I might wear tonight, Clara?" Unravelling the plait she had started, Lilian snatched up the already heated curling-tongs and made gentle cascades of curls. "Something like this?" she asked, hoping Clara would approve.

"That could work, m'lady." Clara gently worked the rest of the hair into torrents of ringlets and then, pulled back the sides in loose braids and finished it with jewelled pins. "Ye look lovely, my lady," Clara offered.

She had to admit, she felt beautiful. "Thank you, Clara, my hair is perfect," she enthused, her tone light as she forgot her now customary diffidence. "I think I am ready."

"You surely are, m'lady. Lord Harlow will have a harder time than usual not to stare at you." Her maid babbled on about her hair while Lilian had already begun to think about dinner. Winston helped her downstairs to the first floor.

Lord Harlow gave an elegant bow when he saw her. "You

are a vision, my lady. May I escort you in to dinner?" Leaning sideways, he whispered softly in her ear.

"I would like that," she replied, happy to see him at last, and thankful that her handicap made no difference to him. Winston stepped aside, allowing Harlow to push her chair into the dining room. Her parents, sister and the Viscount walked ahead of them while Lord Worsley walked alongside.

"We appreciate Lord Avalon's invitation to stay. The accommodations are far better than the fare we received at the inn," he said.

"We are happy to welcome you, my lord," she responded. Lilian noticed she and her sister had been placed across the table from the gentlemen, making it very hard not to stare in their direction.

The first course of turtle soup was removed, but before the servants could carry in the next dishes, her father rose from his chair and sounded his spoon on his wine glass. It had always been his preference as a dinner bell.

"We are very fortunate this evening to have with us Lord Harlow, Lord Worsley and Lord Yarstone. As to that," he paused, smiling happily, "it is my great pleasure to announce the betrothal of my daughter, Lady Lydia DeLacey, to Richard, Viscount Yarstone."

Everyone responded with felicitations of good cheer, clinking their glasses together.

Lilian caught Harlow's eye as her father finished welcoming Viscount Yarstone, and he inclined his head in her direction as the toast proceeded. She was genuinely happy for her sister. Even her own, annoying, green-eyed monster had vanished. There would be a buzz over the upcoming nuptials throughout the village, plus it would give Mama a new focus. The rest of the evening feast comprised plates of fish, boiled meats, mashed potatoes, and a variety of oysters, vegetables and sweetbreads. Desserts filled a small sideboard at the end of the room. With the presence of their guests, Lilian's interest in dinner increased. With the happy news, there was no other focal point for the company. Even Lilian, between bites of food and snippets of conversation, found herself drawn into the preparations for Lydia's wedding and what role she would play in the organization.

When the meal ended, Lord Worsley, Viscount Yarstone and her father retired to his study for the customary glass of port. She was about to join her sister and mother in the parlour, when Harlow approached her and asked to spend a few minutes with her. With Mama's permission, they moved outside on to the veranda, which opened from the dining room, leaving the doors wide open for chaperonage.

The veranda had a smooth stone floor and thick white columns to the ceiling which were interconnected by white wooden railings. Steps led to her mother's garden; filled with colourful flowering bushes, trellises of pink and red roses covered the white fencing that surrounded it. It was a warm evening making Lilian miss even more the ability to walk among the lovely plantings.

Harlow grabbed a white wooden chair that had been resting next to the wall of the house and placed it at a slight angle to Lilian's wheel-chair before taking a seat.

"It was kind of your parents to invite Max and me to stay. Admittedly, it is much more comfortable than the accommodations at the inn in town." A grin pulled at his lips. "I think we are alone, and I do not know how long that will last." He leaned over and brushed her lips softly before then covering her mouth with his own. His tongue tapped on her lips, urging them open.

Lilian tasted the wine which still lingered on his lips and quickly warmed to his kiss. She opened her mouth slightly, and his tongue took advantage, invading the cavity, teasing and caressing her own. Her body began to heat in response.

She closed her eyes, allowing her mind to soar, carried by the delicious scent of bay leaf and bergamot, the fragrance of him she had memorized since the day of her accident. *I have wanted this all evening.* His scent pulled her in, and she kissed him back, her arms softly resting about his neck.

Booted feet walking across the wooden floor of the dining room roused them from the kiss and she pulled back, attempting to regain her composure and slow down her own ragged breathing before they were discovered.

"You look perfectly presentable," he whispered, sitting straighter in his own chair.

Viscount Yarstone and her sister appeared in the doorway. "Would you mind if we joined you?" Yarstone asked.

"Not at all. Please do," Harlow replied. He stood and offered her sister the chair.

"That is very kind," Lydia acknowledged, "but I enjoy leaning over the railings—dreadfully indecorous of me, I know! The scent of honeysuckle is one of my favourites and the perfume is particularly lovely at night."

"Felicitations to the both of you on your engagement." Harlow extended his hand to Yarstone, who shook it heartily.

"Thank you, Harlow," Yarstone replied. "I cannot wait to make Lydia my bride. I have been pinching myself all day to make sure I am not dreaming," he added.

Lydia gave a nervous laugh. "Mama seems overjoyed, and will have a new diversion, although I do rather dread meeting that horrible Lady Poinz again in the village. Why is she even here?"

"What happened, my dear?" Yarstone asked. "I do not believe we have spoken of it."

Lydia related the incident, drawing out every detail of her mother's reproach to the woman.

"Lilian and I were astonished," she declared. "The woman

should have a care. Our Mama can be fierce when she is protecting one of us."

"Was she attacking one of you?" Yarstone asked, raising a brow.

"It seemed to me she was making a point at Lilian's expense. Mama was not about to accept such behaviour and gave Lady Poinz a cutting set-down. I was most impressed."

Lilian grimaced. Mama would be most embarrassed if she heard herself being discussed so.

"Did you, by any chance, see a man wearing black while you were on your walk earlier today?" Lilian ventured to ask.

"What are you speaking of, Lilian? Did you seen such a person?" Harlow asked, his voice tight with some emotion she could not quite determine.

"I thought I saw him earlier today, shortly after they left for a walk," she said, motioning to Lydia and Richard, "but when I asked Mary to look, he had disappeared, assuming he even existed. However, I have never been one to see things that are non-existent. I thought it best to mention it to Father."

"No, I did not see anyone. Did you, Richard?" Lydia asked, concern clear in her voice.

"The only person with us was your maid," responded Yarstone.

After a moment of silence, Yarstone and Lydia returned to the drawing room.

"We are behind you, Lydia," Lilian informed her sister, then releasing the brake on her chair so that Harlow could push it.

Lilian turned her chair to face him. She wished they could stay on the veranda a little longer, but with Lydia and Richard leaving, it was not appropriate.

"Wait. You saw someone watching the house?" he asked, his voice low.

"I thought I did, but he disappeared," she responded, feeling a little unsure now. Perhaps she should not have mentioned it. She felt silly.

"Can you describe him?"

"Not very well. He was too far away. He wore black and had a large blot of black on his face…like a moustache, although it was not clear from the window." Now she was worrying that there *had* been someone.

"One more thing." He lifted up her chin. "You mean a great deal to me. I have work to do in the village tomorrow but would ask you to make sure Winston or your father are with you if you leave the house."

"Should I fear something?" Her throat suddenly felt as though it was closing. Was she in danger?

"I do not think so, but what you have related leaves me concerned. I will return again late tomorrow evening."

"I will do as you say." She wondered if her father had found anything after she had commented on it to him earlier and decided she would ask him in the morning.

Harlow brushed a quick kiss across her lips and pushed her chair towards the parlour.

Mama spoke up at their arrival. "We may have all enjoyed our dinner a little more than usual. We were all about to retire."

"I think I will make an early night of it as well," Harlow replied. "Thank you for a lovely dinner. I believe I will spend what is left of the evening in my bedchamber. Good night." He sketched a bow and left on his words.

Later, Lilian lay awake, thinking about the day. Cooper lay on the pillow next to her and she pulled him closer, nuzzling him. She felt a sense of calmness with Harlow in the house—there was no other way to describe it.

The next morning, Lilian hurried to dress and had Winston bring her downstairs to the breakfast parlour, with

Cooper behind her, to break her fast, hoping she would see Lord Harlow before he and Lord Worsley left. Her father, Lord Worsley, and Lord Harlow were already eating.

"Good morning, daughter." The Earl stood up as Winston eased his daughter's chair to the table, placing her in the empty space to Lord Harlow's left. "Cook has prepared you something special." He gestured to a footman who brought a dish to her and removed the cover.

"Pancakes!" She clapped her hands together. "I whispered to Cook just yesterday that it had been a while since I had enjoyed a good pancake. This is wonderful. With sausage and syrup, it is my favourite!" She looked down at Cooper, who sat patiently looking at her. "I will share a piece with you, sweet boy," she whispered, and tearing off a corner, slid it under the table, hiding it from her father.

"Lilian, the footman placed Cooper's dish in the corner, which is already beyond the bounds of most households," her father chided gently, turning his gaze to the small bowl sitting near the door.

Fancy getting caught, she chastised herself as she felt the warmth of colour stealing up her neck.

"Daughter, I have just been speaking with Lords Harlow and Worsley about the man you saw by the lake yesterday." He put down his fork and spoke softly; a deep frown creased his forehead. "You had not imagined him. Winston and I found fresh footprints in a muddy area at the edge of the lake you described. They could not have been made by your sister or Lord Yarstone, since they were together. These prints were on the smallish side for a man, but they showed the presence of only one person."

Harlow inclined his head in her direction. "Lady Lilian, please stay close to the house until Max and I look into this." His voice was very sombre.

She gave an affirmative nod of her head and looked down

at her chair. "I will do my best. I have not been about the grounds in the last year," she said, struggling to keep self-pity from her voice.

Harlow reached over with his left hand and covered hers for a moment. His touch sent familiar butterflies to her stomach. *What I would give to be closer to him, to place my head on his chest and run my fingers through his hair.* She wanted all of that and much more—so much more that she did not understand.

Lord Worsley looked across the table at Harlow. "We should be on our way, I think."

Harlow finished with his napkin and stood up. "We may be back late tonight, your lordship."

"You have a task to perform. Take your time and get it done to the best of your ability," her father returned.

Lilian knew better than to ask, yet she could not help but wonder what they were doing in Tintagel.

"Are you ready, Cooper? Shall we go to the back portico and play with your ball?" She reached into her pocket and withdrew the blue tethered ball her mother had given her. She showed Cooper, and he jumped on her lap, intent on playing with it. "Please allow us a few minutes to remove from the house." She took her puppy, and the two of them rode together to the portico.

Cooper loves to play ball, she thought. *I wish I had brought the larger one I made. He enjoys shaking it in his teeth until it surrenders,* she chuckled, tossing the ball for her dog.

"I smell smoke, Cooper," she remarked after some minutes of play. She sniffed the air and looked around her, trying to determine what was burning. "The stables! Oh, no!" She rang the bell hanging near her on the portico and frantically wheeled her chair down the path towards the fire. The bricked path her father had made for her sloped slightly down hill, making getting to the stable quicker. Cooper ran ahead of her, barking furiously and repeatedly trying to jump in her lap. He seemed to want her to stop. However, Lilian could only think of her horse, Danby, who would perish in a fire unless released from his stall.

"Barney!" She shouted repeatedly, without response. She wheeled her chair as fast as she could, praying she did not tip, and relieved to see the front of the stable was free of fire. Tears streaming, and calling his name, she manoeuvred her chair towards Danby's stall. The small dog continued to protest. *She would not risk her dog's life, too.*

"Cooper, get help!" She pointed the dog back towards the house. He barked in protest, jumping on her and running towards the door, trying to tell her to come with him, but eventually stopped and ran outside.

Lilian wheeled as fast as she could towards her horse, screaming his name. She could hear fear in his whinny and that of Ginger, her sister's horse. The stable was already overwarm, and the smell of smoke was almost suffocating. She yelled again for Barney and the grooms, but no one answered. The stable was large and could comfortably hold well over two dozen horses when filled. Danby's stall was now about twenty feet ahead. *Where can everyone be?* She pushed the wheels harder, seeing a wall of smoke encroaching from the back of the stable. She had to get to him. The only option was to cut him loose. Reaching the edge of his stall, with no thought for what she was doing, she stood up and leaned against the partition separating Danby's stall from her sister's horse. Her feet dragged unsteadily and after a few steps, she felt too weak to continue. Exhausted and gasping from the smoke, she saw the cane her sister had given her, hanging close enough to reach. She pulled herself closer to the partition and stretched to reach the cane…until, at last, she was able to lift it from the wall. Leaning heavily on it, Lilian pushed herself to walk. *Just a few steps, please.*

Awkwardly, she struggled along his stall towards the manger. Finally getting close enough, she reached over and freed Danby from his tether. Her horse whinnied louder and began nudging her with his head to climb on him. Gagging from the smoke, she steadied herself and tore off a section of her gown. Soaking it in his bucket of water, she then fashioned it over her nose and mouth.

"Run, Danby!" she ordered, but her horse would not leave. *What is wrong with him?* The horse grabbed the fabric of her gown in his teeth and backed up, trying to drag her from the stall. *I cannot leave Ginger.* With every last ounce of strength, she pulled herself up on the cane and inched around the wall that separated them, disengaging the chain across the heel end of the stall and reaching for Ginger's rope and finally unhooking her headstall. The mare ran towards the open door, but still Danby stayed. Instead, he pushed her with his nose and stamped his hooves. *Could he want her to climb on him?* Lilian dearly wanted to try, except her strength faltered, and again, she screamed for him to go. Still, he remained. Desperate, she looked for her chair, but it was almost ten feet away. It might as well have been halfway across the sea. The fire had grown too close. Fire licked at the thick ceiling beams and the thick smoke billowed towards them, choking and almost blinding her. Fearing the roof would soon cave in, Lilian dropped to her stomach and crawled towards her chair, encouraged only by the soft nickers of her horse and the continued pushes of his nose.

The pounding of footsteps and Cooper's barks closed in on Lilian's fading senses. Then she felt herself being scooped up into warm arms and held tightly against a muscled chest.

"I have you, Lilian. Stay with me! You are safe now. I will never let you go." Harlow's voice broke, but she warmed to it.

"Is my daughter still breathing?" It was her father's ragged voice. She heard other male voices, frantically issuing orders and saying her name. She wanted to answer but could not.

"Yes, thank God. She still breathes."

"We moved Barney on to the grass beyond the yard and have sent for the doctor."

Warm teardrops fell on her face, and she fluttered her eyes. "My dog, my horse…?"

"They saved your life, my dearest one. They are safe. Thank God we got to you in time." Harlow pulled her close against him.

Her nostrils burned from the acrid smoke, yet she could still smell his pleasing scent. His heartbeat thumped powerfully against her ear.

"I am safe," she muttered hoarsely, and closed her eyes.

CHAPTER 16

Harlow and Max had gathered necessary supplies for the day and were heading out of the door to collect their horses. Lord Avalon had generously asked Cook to provide some sandwiches, fruits, and cheeses for the three men, while they waited for the operation to take place. Winston opened the door for them, and Lilian's dog shot through his legs and ran to Harlow, barking madly. The small dog repeatedly jumped up against his leg and then ran a short distance in front of him until the men realized the puppy wanted them to follow. As soon as they were clear of the doorway, Harlow smelled acrid smoke of a fire.

"The stables are on fire!" Max pointed towards a plume of grey-black smoke.

"Get Lord Avalon," Harlow turned and shouted to Winston before running behind Max down the brick path. The two men hastened after the dog, which had calmed a little and was racing ahead. The back of the stables was burning, the roof ablaze with orange flame and thick smoke, and with no back door to the stables, the black smoke was bellowing forth. Cooper had been alone, and Lilian was nowhere to be seen. In sudden horror, Harlow realized that Lilian was probably in there. Panting more from fear than exertion, they charged into the stable yard and met a young groom who had moved as many horses as possible out into the paddocks.

They found Barney unconscious, and his body pulled behind a blanket chest in the harness room. The large lantern was still hanging in the entrance, but he had already suspected the cause was one of the ones along the passage fronting the stalls. As if of one mind, both men took off their shirts, soaked them in a nearby trough and held them over their heads. Lord Avalon and Yarstone arrived as they began to fight their way through the acrid smoke and at once did the same.

Harlow recalled that Danby's stall was closer to the feed room and away from the fire. As he and the other men ventured into the burning structure, they met a groom shooing his and Max's horses from the back of the stable and breathed a sigh of relief. Several male servants from the house had also run in to help with the horses, and Max called a servant to run for the veterinarian.

"Have you seen Lady Lilian?" Harlow asked loudly. The groom shook his head.

"I 'asn't seen Barney, neither. Had to get these 'orses out afore I looked, sir. There are still two more horses in 'ere. I started at the far end, see, nearest the fire." The man pointed toward the stalls at the other end of the row, where Danby was housed.

A ginger-coloured mare ran past them, followed by sounds of a horse still in distress. The men ran towards the sound of stamping. Then they heard a woman scream. The piercing sound came from the direction of Danby's stall. Harlow chased along the passage as though he had wings. He found Lilian on the ground, her horse alternately nudging her and tugging at her skirts, clearly trying to drag her towards the door. In her right hand she clutched a wooden cane.

Thinking her dead, Harlow picked her up and pulled her close to his heart, begging her not to leave him. The sight of her hair hanging dirty and limp around her shoulders caused his heart to sink. He ripped off the wet rag covering her nose and mouth and willed her to breathe. He could see the rise and fall of her chest, albeit slightly; it gave him hope. She tried to open her eyes but could only mouth his name. Rogue tears escaped unchecked down his face.

"Is my daughter still breathing?" her father cried out, grasping her face and begging her to open her eyes.

"My dog, my horse?" she muttered.

Harlow wanted to get down on his knees and give thanks. If he had not been holding her, he would have done so. Slowly, he turned and carried her out into the fresh air. Only then did he realize his state of undress. Feeling a surge of embarrassment, he looked away over the paddock fences, where the horses were grazing, rolling and kicking up their heels in happy freedom. Miraculously, all the animals had survived the blaze, because of the quick thinking of the groom and the strength and will of this beautiful woman in his arms.

Max brought up Lilian's chair, also largely unscathed, and with great reluctance, Harlow lowered her into it. A few moments later, a large crash sounded as part of the roof towards the back of the stable fell. He shielded her body as sparks leaped into the air.

Viscount Yarstone had organized two bucket brigades to douse the flames from two directions and wetting the ground surrounding the stable. A fire engine finally arrived from the village and directed its efforts on the centre of the blaze, fuelled by unspent ceiling timbers. It took several more hours before the estate workers could get the blaze under control, to a point where they finally felt it could burn itself out.

The doctor, who had arrived earlier, said, "Keep her propped up with pillows to enable her lungs to function more easily. I have told her maid. The posture will assist in forcing out the poisons inhaled from the smoke. I will return in a day or two to see how she goes on." Lifting his hat to the assembled servants, family and well-wishers, he had departed.

She could have died. A shudder of fear shook Harlow as he realized how close she had come to death, and how close he had come to losing the person he needed to share his life. A groom had reported seeing a lantern thrown into one of the back stalls, confirming their suspicions that the fire had been no accident.

Harlow hated to leave Lilian, but duty demanded it. The ride to the cave was quiet for much of the way. By the time Harlow and Max arrived, the Dragoon Captain Newman had already had him take up a position out of the sight of any townsfolk or passers-by.

"It is good to see you, m'lord. Thank you for your notice. I have my men in place," Captain Newman stated. "They have their sights on the opening where we expect the skirmish and are ready to arrest the conspirators."

"Be alert for two people," Max cut in. "A man with a dark moustache who will, most likely, be garbed in black. The other one is Lady Catherine Poinz. We believe them to be the accomplice and the ringleader—or else closely in league with them."

"The widow Poinz?" Newman paled.

"Yes. Is there something we should know, Captain?"

Harlow asked in a menacing tone. DeLacey heard the exchange and moved closer. "If you have something to say, say it. Lives are at stake, not just a boat and its booty."

"I may have seen her early this morning, riding a horse. We had hidden, so she did not see us, but had we known she was a focal point of this operation, we would have held her for questioning."

Harlow breathed a sigh of relief. He had been afraid Newman would say he had spoken to her or that she had seen him. If she knew they were watching, she would cancel everything. Relief was clear on Max's and DeLacey's faces, too.

"Where did you say you saw her?" he persisted.

"She was riding like the wind towards the coast. I cannot be sure where she had been, but it was clear she was determined to get somewhere fast."

Not sure what to make of that, Harlow and Max looked at each other.

"What was she wearing?" Max asked.

"A yellow gown and a black hat with a feather, although the hat was barely hanging on her head. She appeared to have it secured with a ribbon about her neck.

"Send word to your men, if you will. Tell them we need the pair for questioning, nothing more. Thank you for your information," Max finished, dismissing the Captain.

"Cressey, we need to talk to you," Harlow said, his face set, "in private."

DeLacey's cave was most elaborate. Small holes, covered loosely by brushwood, allowed light to filter from the top, although he was not sure those were not the result of the weather and the sea unleashing its vengeance on the cliff's sides. If a person stepped on a hole from above, they could wedge their foot and break an ankle. However, the chances of that happening seemed remote. He was correct in his assertion that no one had used the cave in years. A colony of bats flew past them as they walked deeper, looking for a place of privacy. Sparse light, offered by the small holes in the top, allowed them to adjust their vision more readily.

"This looks like a good spot," Max remarked.

"What is it you have to say? Does it have anything to do with the two of you being late?" DeLacey snapped, his tone critical. "This should all start to unfold in a few hours,"

Harlow stepped up and looked him squarely in the eye. "Your sister almost died in a stable fire, along with your head groom and the horses."

The air whooshed out of DeLacey, and he staggered. "Is she well?" His voice trembled.

At least the man cares for his family, Harlow reflected. "Yes, she is. You have not met him, but a small puppy she rescued, a little more than a week past, saved her life. It may sound fantastical, yet the truth is, he and her horse both did," Harlow explained.

"They all saved each other," Max put in. "We were convinced the widow's man was responsible…or we were until Captain Newman shared his information. The widow would have had access to the estate at the time of the fire, and she was coming from that direction. Motive is the only loose string."

"Motive? The woman *hates* my family. I should rather say she hates my mother." DeLacey drew in air between his teeth, almost hissing. "I should have been there."

"We were there, and that did not stop this from happening." Max paused. "May we ask why there is acrimony between them? It is important. Your mother and the widow had what I would describe as an impassioned exchange yesterday morning, in town. She was directing her remarks to Lady Lilian and your mother interceded."

DeLacey inclined his head. "Once upon a time, she threw

her cap at my father. Their parents were acquaintances and had always spoken of the two becoming betrothed, but my father met my mother and any betrothal to the widow ran aground," DeLaney explained. "In the end, she married a man as old as her own father, who, while rich, was not what she had wished for. She coveted being a Countess as much as being wealthy. Keep in mind this is my father's account. There could be more."

"That matches with my theory. I believe the widow singled out your sister when she saw Lady Lilian had caught the fancy of Lord Harlow, here. He may not want to acknowledge it, but many women dangle after him." Max's lips turned up in a slight smile.

"God's teeth, Max!" Harlow said, glowering at his friend. "Are you responsible for the bet at White's?"

"No, be easy. You know it was not me. Nonetheless, I believe we will determine who did that shortly."

"What do you mean?" DeLacey demanded. "What bet? Did it involve my sister?" The man's face darkened with anger. "How dare anyone place my sister's name in the betting books!"

"I believe I know who it was, but let us see," Max said coolly.

Harlow appreciated Max's coolness under fire. They were like that with each other. When he got upset, Max calmed him. When Max flew up into the boughs, he calmed his friend.

"Your father sent us food. Shall we eat now before this begins? I think this would be a good spot," Harlow suggested mildly.

A few hours later, the men were in place with their pistols primed and their knives ready. The Dragoons would be their first line of defence, but they planned to have the widow and her associate in custody, regardless of who apprehended her.

Harlow now knew that DeLacey shared a second motivation to make sure she paid. *His sister.*

Darkness surrounded them, and for more than an hour, no one moved. Harlow checked his brass pocket-watch, closing it and making the loudest sound they had heard in hours. Barely beyond King's Cave, a lantern edged out on the water, a clear decoy set in place to lead Lieutenant Pelham's cutter onto the jagged coastal rocks. The lantern was most likely on a small boat being floated or manoeuvred by long ropes. They had seen the small black dinghy hidden under brushwood on the coast. It was the chief means used by free traders to access the cargo once they wrecked a boat. The black colour helped conceal them.

Pelham's cutter edged into the opening, straying closer to the rocks. *Be careful.* Harlow was worried; anything could go wrong. He pulled out his spyglass and watched, barely making out a cutter purposely camouflaged in black, flanking Pelham's larboard side.

A noise on the beach drew his attention. A man dressed in black stood off to the side, barely visible beside the dark boulder he leaned on. Harlow looked carefully and saw him withdraw a silver pistol. Using an agreed-upon signal, he lit a match and made a quick flash, barely seen by an unsuspecting eye. The man appeared preoccupied with Pelham's ship and as far as Harlow could tell, did not notice. He could see villagers and smugglers edging toward the shore, staying close to the cliff's edge until the British ship lay crippled on the rocks.

As the black cutter drew closer, attempting to box Pelham's ship, forcing it to wreck, five guns fired from the British cutter, making direct hits on the smuggler's boat and crippling her masts. Flames erupted from several areas on the boat, and judging from the chaos that ensued, the smugglers' ship was crippled and on fire.

Dragoons swarmed the beach, fighting those that resisted arrest. They had not planned to arrest the townspeople, but they wanted the leaders.

Harlow looked down and realized the man in black was slowly edging away. *He is trying to escape.* Standing up, Harlow looked down to the side, spotting the man just below his own hiding place. The man was climbing the rock in an attempt to flee for safety. Harlow tucked his pistol into his belt and leaped from the rocks screening their vantage point, landing on top of the man. Before Harlow could secure bindings, the man slipped an arm free and pulled out a short knife and cut through Harlow's shirt, lacerating his shoulder. The assailant then had time to climb a rocky outcrop and somersault in front Harlow, with a small flintlock pistol drawn.

"You had better make that shot count, because you will not get a second chance..."

The man glanced behind Harlow. In that instant, Harlow seized his chance and wrestled the man to the ground. The pistol discharged into the air. Max appeared next to him and kicked the gun away.

"We did not see the widow, but he will talk," Max remarked.

"He will do more than that," Harlow growled. DeLacey came into view just as Harlow ripped the coarse black moustache from the man's face.

"What are you doing? The Prince Regent..." DeLacey stopped mid-sentence.

"The Prince will recognize the widow." Harlow finished the sentence for him.

As one, Max and DeLacey exhaled loudly in disbelief.

"She was *both* of them," DeLacey murmured. "How did you know?"

"I recognized the feel of a woman's chest. Never have I

known a man to have breasts." He half-laughed at his own remark, but he was serious. His anger with this woman for what she had tried to do to Lilian was ungovernable.

"Excellent work, gentlemen," Captain Newman boomed as he approached the little group.

None too gently, Harlow bound the widow's wrists and handed her into the Captain's care.

"This was one of the smoothest operations I have ever been a part of, gentlemen. We have several individuals we feel had a hand in leading this smuggling ring, and we plan to take them in for questioning. We did not see the widow…" he said, stopping mid-sentence. *"He is her."* Newman looked confused as he stared at the bedraggled prisoner, now tied up in front of them.

"Does anyone have a handkerchief?" Harlow asked.

"I do." DeLacey handed him a fine silk handkerchief. Harlow forced the widow's mouth open and stuffed the cloth into it.

"No one wants to hear any of her nastiness."

"I have this in hand now, Harlow. Thank you both. You can make your reports. Mayhap you would be more comfortable back at the inn." DeLacey winked and lowered his voice to a whisper. "Let my father know I will see him tomorrow."

"Very good, Cressey." Harlow brushed the sand off his clothing and gathering their belongings, the two men rode back to Elysium Manor.

"Now that Cressey…DeLacey…is not here, tell me who you think placed that bet in the Betting Book at White's," Harlow said to his friend. He was not as angry as he had initially been, but it rankled that someone would place Lilian's name in such a book.

"I will answer your question with a question." Max said smugly. "'Tis easy enough if you think who may have felt threatened the most by your association with the DeLacey twins."

Could Max be right? "You do not think he is associated with…?"

"No, no. I think it was a simple case of jealousy," Max interrupted. "Keep in mind, I was not there, but you have related enough of the exchanges around Lady Lilian DeLacey, that I think it is where the guilt lies. We will not know for sure until we ask."

The two men fed and watered their horses and walked up to the house. Harlow's priorities were news of Lilian, sleep and food, in that order. Hearing that she was resting comfortably, he relaxed. He needed to think more, but the minute his head hit the pillow he went to sleep, comfortable knowing that the next day held an excitement all its own.

EPILOGUE

he next day

Lilian lay in bed with her eyes closed, feeling the sun warm her face. She was trying to have a better dream to wake up with so she might rid her mind of a most unsettling nightmare. In her nightmare, the stable had caught fire, trapping over a dozen horses, including her horse and her sister's horse, nearly burning them alive. She adored Danby, and the idea she could lose him to something so devastating shook her to the core. Try as she might, she could not reach him. When she did at last free him, he refused to leave her side. With her remaining strength depleted, she collapsed, able neither to save herself nor her animals. Somewhere in her dream she could smell him, the Prince Charming her sister had continually promised would come for her. The scent of bergamot and bay leaf filled her mind, and she felt her face relax, content that he had swooped in and saved them all. Part of her believed it had been a dream, and all of her wished the last part had been true. Experience had taught her that if she stayed asleep, she could find herself in a better reverie, freeing her consciousness of this horrible dream.

A knock sounded on her bedchamber door, shattering any chance for a daydream. Slowly, she opened her eyes to see her sister kiss her on the forehead and plop into a chair next to her.

"I love you so much, dear sister. If not for you, I would not have my precious Ginger."

"Then it was true," she said through a lump in her throat. The horrific part of her dream was not a dream, after all. It was a bad memory coming back larger than ever.

"The fire? Yes, but so much has happened. Do you remember using the cane?" Her sister's voice nearly burst with excitement.

I used a cane, she remembered. "Yes." Her voice hitched. "I could not get close enough to the horses. Then I saw the cane you left there for me, so I walked to it." Of their own volition, her lips formed an 'O'. Sitting up, she threw her covers back. "I walked? I walked!" She reached for her legs and could feel her hands touching her skin. She had not felt her legs in a year.

"Yes. *All* of that!" Tears ran unchecked down Lydia's face and she buried her face in her sister's shoulder. "I love you," she mumbled, her voice muffled by Lilian's hair. "You are my hero, sister."

"Yes, she is," Mama said, walking into the room at that moment. "I should be angry with you for what you did, risking your life, but I cannot be. The doctor said you will recover—more than recover, in actual fact. He believes you are ready to enjoy a normal life again."

Mama sounded anything but angry. Maybe the right word was giddy? While she respected her family, Lilian knew, without a doubt, she would do everything to save her animal—even risking her life again, given the circumstances.

"You will want to get dressed soon and break your fast," her mother suggested pointedly. A knowing smile teased her lips.

Cooper bounded into the room and leaped onto her bed, licking the faces of both girls and sending them into giggles.

"I love you, little man. If my nightmare was true, it is you who saved me—you and Danby."

"He is a little rascal, that one." As she mentioned her former dog's name, her mother smiled again. This time it was wistful. "I cut myself off from other dogs, thinking they could not bring back the happiness I had known with my dear little Rascal. Had I refused a home to this puppy, I might have lost my daughter." She leaned down and hugged Cooper, who licked her squarely on the nose. She wiped her nose, then laughed. "I could get used to that again! I have a treat for you," she said, petting Cooper's head and watching him gobble up the biscuit. "I reminded Cook of the salmon-flavoured biscuits she used to make for Rascal, and she made some for Cooper."

"Thank you, Mama," Lilian breathed.

"Tell her what the doctor said," urged Lydia.

Mama cupped Lilian's face affectionately. "The doctor said you should walk again. The accident last year may have created some kind of injurious condition, producing a fear you could not recover from. He is uncertain, as they are just seeing this type of occurrence with all the war injuries. The doctor thinks the fear of losing your beloved horse forced you to move past the affright which was causing your paralysis. He spoke in terms I did not understand completely. However, I grasped that you will walk again." She stood up, wiping away fresh tears. "Get dressed." She walked over to the bell and pulled it. "I shall see you downstairs."

Thirty minutes later, Lilian met Lord Harlow and Lord Worsley as they were leaving her father's study. Both gentlemen gave a quick bow. She noticed Lord Worsley's sly grin as he excused himself and slipped away in the direction of the dining room.

"Good morning, Lilian." Harlow leaned down and whispered in her ear, "Will you join me in the parlour for a few minutes?"

She looked and judged the parlour to be only ten feet in front of her. Reaching behind her chair, she grabbed the cane her sister had given her and tested it on the floor in front of her before easing herself up. Awkwardly, she pushed one foot forward and, once stable, dragged forward the other one. The steps got easier as she moved to the doorway of the room.

Harlow stood just beyond the entry to the room, gaping and wiping rogue tears from his eyes. "I never thought I would see…how is this possible?" he asked, shock registering on his face. "Lilian…you are walking." His voice shook with emotion. "Are you tired? Do you wish to continue?" Harlow swiped at his cheeks but was unable to stem the tears rolling unchecked down his face.

Unsure of her stamina, but determined to try, she replied, "I do." Her movement was jerky, but with every step she accomplished, the smile on her face widened. When she reached the settee, she turned and sat down—or, more accurately, plopped down.

"Lilian…" he started to speak but stopped. Changing his mind, instead Harlow kneeled down in front of her and took her hand, looking up into her face.

She was not sure what had prompted her efforts to walk, but Lilian had not expected this. Her throat constricted with emotion as she beheld John's tear-stained face. She at once felt elated, captivated and cherished as a myriad of implausible emotions washed over her.

"Lady Lilian DeLacey, I beg you, make me the happiest of men and say you will become my Countess. Having almost lost you, I have realized I cannot live without you. I *love* you." Harlow whispered the last words to her, barely getting the last word out before she heard low murmurs coming from the doorway. Overcome, she glanced up.

Her sister, Viscount Yarstone, Lord Worsley, her parents, Clara, Winston and Chambers stood crowded in the doorway, smiles filling their faces. Cooper squeezed beneath their legs and came into the room. Lying down in front of her, he gazed up at her face.

"Yes," she whispered. "Yes, John Andrews, Earl of Harlow, I will marry you—on the condition that I be allowed to walk down the aisle to your arms." She shook her curls. "Since nothing about this engagement appears to be fashionable standards, I think I should like to do it this way."

"This is where you all are! There was no one at the door to take my coat and I thought something had happened." The group parted, and her brother joined them.

"You have missed nothing, Jonathan, except our sister's engagement," Lydia said, giving him a hug.

"Your attention, please, everyone," Father spoke up. "Lilian and Lord Harlow are now engaged, and it is permissible to allow them a few minutes alone. What do you say we all go to the dining room and break our fast together?"

"Thank you, sir. All except one, I believe. Viscount Yarstone, please stay a moment longer. I have something to ask you," Harlow said quietly. When the others had left, he turned to Yarstone. "Max read out to me a bet in White's—the substance of which no longer upsets me. However, I need to know the truth. Did you place it there?"

Yarstone paled. "I…I apologize. It was a foolish whim.

'Twas a ridiculous pierce of jealousy. Can you ever forgive me...?"

"Say no more. I believe I now understand. I just wanted to know. It drove me crack-brained." He winked and patted Yarstone on the back. "To make amends, I ask that you consider allowing us to have a double wedding. What say you?"

"I say, yes indeed and well done! A double wedding it is, providing the family is in agreement," Yarstone answered.

"I think Mama and Father will be happy with it—more than happy, in fact. They will love it!" Lilian agreed at once.

"If that is all, I shall join them for breakfast." Bowing, Yarstone left quickly and, followed by Cooper, pulled the door closed."

Lilian looked up into the eyes of the man in front of her. She had found her Prince Charming.

"I think I am the happiest of people and the very luckiest."

He pulled her from the couch and held her, brushing her lips with his softly and then covering her mouth with his and hugging her to his chest.

Lilian found his kisses and caresses exciting, and melted into them, enraptured with his hunger and need of her.

"I think our lives together shall never be dull."

Lilian looked into his eyes, her own overflowing with tears. "John, you are the prince my sister promised I would find. You are all I could have imagined—all I have ever imagined. I love you." She pulled his lips to her own and kissed him with all the emotion she possessed. This morning she had awoken afraid of her nightmare, only to realize it was the true beginning to her life and all her wishes were about to come true.

AFTERWORD

***Please note:* This book is written using *historic* British English spellings and grammar to better reflect the time period of the story. For example, *favour* is used instead of favor, *parlour* is used instead of parlor, *marvellous* instead of marvelous, *colour* instead of color, *wheel-chair* instead of wheelchair. These are correct spellings.**

THE EARL SHE LEFT BEHIND
CHAPTER 1

Maidstone, Kent, England
October 1815

Thunder boomed above him. A second later, a sharp crack of lightning lit up the dark sky. Gripping the reins of his horse, Maxwell Wilde, Earl of Worsley, fought to stay seated as his mare reared and struggled. The lightning illuminated a woman lying in the road just ahead. Had the lightning not struck, he most certainly would not have seen her.

The scant light showed a small-framed woman curled into a fetal position, wearing a soiled blue dress. A small shaggy white dog pawed her arm, whimpering and licking her face. Large drops of rain pelted both of them but did not affect the dog's loyal persistence.

"Whoa, Willow." Max slid from his mount and walked over to the woman. At his approach, the dog at once became protective, giving a guttural growl. It forced Max to stop and rethink his goal.

"Easy, boy." He lowered his hand to the dog and allowed him to sniff it. The dog stopped growling and eased himself down, curling his furry white body next to the woman's head—protecting her—still whimpering and licking her face. Max took a deep breath, careful not to anger the dog and not wanting to injure it. The dog was unmistakably attached to the woman. Feeling more confident the dog would not attack him, he lowered himself onto his haunches to get a better look at the woman.

Gently, he swept wet, muddied blonde tresses from her face. Recognition was swift and tumultuous. "Bloody hell! Meg, what happened? Why are you out in this storm, of all places? Why are you here?" Questions flooded his brain. He fought the gut-wrenching impulse to pull her close. When she did not answer, he picked up a limp hand and noticed rope burns around her left wrist, anger registering. "You are bleeding." He moved her damp blonde hair away from her forehead, revealing a deep gash from which blood still oozed. Fear gripped him. He stared at her motionless body until he saw her chest barely move. Good. She was breathing. "Thank goodness you are still alive."

Her eyes opened and closed. Her throat worked, but she did not speak. She needed a doctor. Max needed to get her to safety and leave before she engaged his heart yet again.

He had washed his hands of Maggie Winters when she ran away and abruptly married the Earl of Tipton three years past—when she and Max were planning to wed. Anger churned in his gut as he thought about the day he found out, and it renewed his confusion, pain, and anger. She had disappeared without a word—merely a scribbled note delivered to him. Without thinking, he reached inside this waistcoat pocket and touched the folded missive. No one had heard from Maggie in years. It was strange, but word of her marriage had cleared it up for him. He squashed the now-familiar feeling of dread.

"No, no, no! Leave him alone! Please…do not harm him." Her voice was hoarse and barely audible. She rolled her head from left to right and moved her hands about herself in defense—defending against what, he did not understand. Was she speaking about the small dog? With one eye on Max, the dog was furiously licking her face. He was trying to calm her. *Amazing.*

The small animal gave a sharp bark, trying to gain her attention. "Rrrr…uff."

Unsure of the dog's reaction to his presence, he increased the space between them. He had no wish to have an animal of any size bite him. But the bark itself triggered an awareness. He vaguely recalled having met this animal. But when? He narrowed his eyes, attempting to remember. It had been a while since he had seen Meg. She could have gained a pet without his notice. It had been three years since he had last laid eyes on her.

The heaviness in his heart was returning. Max had tried to forget her. He wanted to forget her. The last thing he needed was to be in her presence now. But Meg's condition terrified him. Ignoring her was not an option. He smoothed the wet hair away from the sides of her face.

Lifting her, he placed her on his saddle. Her body slumped. He leaned in close, holding her against his shoulder, then put his left foot in the stirrup and hoisted himself up behind her. He held her gently in case there was any other injury he had not seen. The touch of her sent his pulse racing, but Max did his best to hold on to Meg and the reins. The dog started barking and jumping, almost bouncing, desperate to gain access to his mistress. Willow twisted and bared her teeth at the dog, as if to tell him to stop, but the small animal was unfazed. He would have to bring the dog.

This dog means something to Meg. Recognition almost knocked him out of his seat. This bedraggled white dog was the same grubby puppy they had saved moments before an out-of-control wagon and its horses would have ended its life, only weeks before Meg had disappeared from his. His heart sped with excitement that she had kept it all this time. "I know you!" He looked down at the dog. "It is coming back to me now." Excited, he leaned into Meg. "I recognize Shep. You kept the dog!" he whispered, realizing she would not hear him but needing to speak. Overwhelmed, he pulled her tight to his chest and breathed in her essence. Lilacs. His favorite. He loved that she always smelled of lilacs. Once upon a time, she told him it was her preferred flower.

The dog waited. Its demeanor communicated the anticipation of accommodation. "I will not leave you. Give me a moment to think." He was speaking almost to himself. It was a difficult position. Thinking rapidly, he reached behind him for his saddlebag and emptied its contents. Nothing of importance was in there. Once satisfied with the space, he carefully slid off his horse, keeping one hand holding onto Meg. She did not move. Hurriedly, he gathered the small dog into the satchel. Shep gave no resistance. Max hoisted the bags over his shoulder to allow the small dog to ride, and once again mounted Willow.

"Shep," she murmured, barely conscious. Her voice was weak. "Shep, where are you?" She tried to open her eyes, but they fluttered closed again.

A lighter bark registered under his arm. He could not believe his ears. The dog had answered her. It *understood* her.

Willow turned into Max's estate and stopped at the front. It had been six months since his last visit home. Still securing Meg with one hand, he slid from his horse, and lowered his saddlebag, allowing the dog to leave it. Then he turned back and gently helped Meg down.

"Follow me." He nodded at the dog, confident the pooch understood him. Holding Meg in his arms, he and the bedraggled pup made it up the steps to the portico and pushed open the door.

The slow but pronounced footfalls of his butler sounded a welcome.

"Your lordship, you have returned. We had not expected you this evening." The tall, greying man drew closer and peered down at the drenched woman in his arms. "I apologize for ogling, my lord, but that is Miss Maggie…pardon, *Lady* Maggie…" He looked up at Max. "Lady Tipton." Max noted the shock and concern in the old man's eyes. "She appears injured. What happened, my lord?" Before Max could answer, the older man noticed the small dog standing at Max's feet and scowled. "Shoo! Out the door with you."

Shep sprung into the air, jumping vertically toward his mistress and barking his high-pitched bark. The energy the dog still had despite the frigid conditions he had endured astonished Max. "It's okay, Cabot. Lady..." He paused, grappling for words. "Lady Tipton needs the dog as much as he needs her. He stays."

"As you wish, my lord. I will send for the doctor." His displeasure clear, Cabot left the room, but not before giving a quick glare toward the dog.

"Thank you, Cabot," he responded under his breath to the man's back. Louder, he added, "Send for Mrs. Andrews and have her meet me upstairs. I shall put Lady…Tipton in Lady Angela's room." Uttering her married name renewed the ache in his chest. He needed to get her help and then distance himself. Angela, his sister, would not mind Meg using her room while she visited her best friend in London. Angela would be gone for at least two more weeks.

It would not be easy to forget Meg's marriage status with

three years past, but he had to for his sanity. And he needed to stop calling her Meg. That had been his nickname for her. She was Lady Maggie Tipton now. Even as he told himself this, he knew it would be impossible—she would always be Meg to him.

Meg's body quaked, probably from the chill. Responding on impulse, Max pulled her closer, hoping to share his body warmth in the only way he knew. She was lighter than he recalled. Her lilac scent rushed his senses and reminded him sharply of his loss. Weirdly, he recalled a time or two he had carried her. Rapt in the past, he missed a step, barely catching himself before he lost his balance.

"Woof!" The dog ran past him up the stairs and stopped at the top. He watched Max the rest of the way up, his expression one of mistrust.

"I promise not to hurt her." *No, I will be the one in pain here,* Max reflected. "It is just ahead, Shep." Good God! He was talking to a dog. Shaking off the realization, he nodded toward the hall. Shep started in behind him, following him into the room. Once inside, Max laid Meg on the pink velvet-covered bed.

Shep jumped up and sniffed at her face, assuring himself she was still alive. Once satisfied, he inspected each of the four large posters before curling up next to her side. Not close enough, his little body edged toward her until it touched her.

"Shep, you have come back," she uttered, weakly placing her hand on his folded front paws with a loud sigh.

Was that relief? His gaze shifted to the burns on her wrists, and he knew he could not dismiss her again from his life so quickly. *I need to know what happened to her.* The burns on Meg's wrists bothered him as much as her tortured state of mind. Was she running from someone…or maybe *to* something? Whatever it was, the dog had a part in it. He had found her in front of her family's estate. Wyndham was almost a mile from his own property.

He had planned to ask for her hand, but a carriage accident claimed the lives of both of her parents the very day he had planned to see her father. Everyone had expected them to marry—he had made his feelings about Maggie clear. He loved her and thought the feeling was mutual. But two days after the funeral for her parents, Maggie Winters had disappeared, leaving only the note.

Her uncle, Silas Winters, had become her guardian, inheriting her father's title of viscount and his entitled properties. Max knew Silas for his gambling and questionable business dealings. Meg had been most unhappy to learn he was to be her guardian until she turned one and twenty.

Wyndham had been her mother's childhood home, but the Winters family had lived there most of the time. Following the death of his brother, Viscount Silas Winters had boarded up the property, never sending a soul to care for it. Max's mother had written that recent sightings of a woman in white staring from the attic window had renewed the rumor that the estate was haunted.

He took a deep breath and gazed at the sleeping woman in front of him. Three years had passed. Max had buried her memory, pushing it to the back of his mind, but seeing her tonight, holding her, and smelling her essence brought painful memories of his loss to the forefront. He had met with her uncle to ask for her hand, and the contracts were being drawn up when Maggie Winters had left town, suddenly marrying a much older Fergus Anders, Earl of Tipton. She had left Max's life with no explanation. Cornered, her uncle would only say he had signed a contract. Nothing more. Max felt he would never know the truth, only the note she left him. The rumors, which were hard to believe, only added salt to his wounded heart.

The gossip was that Meg's uncle had married her to Tipton to settle a gambling loss. Both were notorious gamblers, and the thought that Meg had been taken away unwillingly only added deeper angst. Max had never been sure of what had happened, but he could not reach her, despite his best efforts. With no contract signed, he had no chance of winning her back—if that had even been what had happened. He had heard nothing from her. The loss had decimated Max's heart. He had sworn to never love again, but now he realized he had never stopped loving her. He left town shortly after she did, not willing or able to endure the pity of being jilted by the one person he loved more than life itself.

I can never let her know my feelings.

Max shook his head, hoping to pull himself from his misery. *She is Tipton's wife, yet she is here. Why?* He pulled up one of his sister's pink velvet slipper chairs and sat next to her. "Meg, why are you here now? What happened to you?" The dog opened his eyes and stared at him, never lifting his head. A low, guttural growl erupted.

"I will not hurt her." Max reached tentatively and stroked the cotton-soft hair on the dog's head. Shep allowed it and sniffed his hand. A slight wag of his tail replaced the growl. *Good. He recognizes me.* "Good boy."

Meg's quick wit and sense of adventure had been something he always enjoyed. They got along better together than his school friends, and he had continually enjoyed coming home to her. There was always one scrape or another, and he was always rescuing her—until he could not.

Female voices and the swishing of skirts drew his attention to the door as his mother entered.

"My dear, Cabot mentioned that you had brought Lady Tipton in from an accident. I quickly allowed my guests to leave and came to help." She looked at the prone form in her daughter's bed. "I had to see for myself."

"Mother, thank you. I had not realized you would be here. I thought you were in London for the Season. I am sorry about your guests, but…" He glanced down at Meg. "I found her like this on my way home. She was in front of her parents' gate. With the dog." He nodded at Shep. "That is the dog Meg and I found shortly before…" He took a deep breath. "Shortly before we were to be wed."

"I recall that incident. You could have both died saving the rascal." She smiled at that dog. "I rarely allow dogs in my home, but he seems harmless. I will plan for a bath and some food for him." She sniffed in Shep's direction. "Immediately."

"Lord Worsley, the doctor should be here in a few minutes. Cabot sent the footman for him straightaway." Mrs. Andrews tapped him lightly on the arm.

"Son, I will take over. You change out of those wet clothes." His mother placed her hands on his shoulders and squeezed lightly.

Nodding, Max agreed. "I shall change and be right back." His hand lightly grazed Maggie's. "It would be best not to move her further until the doctor examines her. She has burns on her wrists, and I am most concerned there could be hidden injuries."

"My God! She does." His mother said, her tone one of alarm as she gently rolled Maggie's wrist and leaned in to look more closely. "They appear to be rope burns. Who would have placed ropes on Maggie?"

Shep lifted his head and started to growl, but a sharp, reproachful look from his mother squelched that. Max swallowed a chuckle as he started to leave.

"It is Shep, is it not?" His mother's inquiry stopped him.

"Yes. You recall that? I almost did not recognize him. He

is a protective little chap." He walked over and ruffled the dog's head affectionately.

"I do." She smiled. "I confess, these last three years, I have had a hard time thinking of her as Lady Tipton. She was to be my daughter, but she has not been part of society. I just can't imagine..." Her voice trailed off as her hand gently moved a little wet and bloodied hair from Meg's face. "Something drastic has happened. We shall help her all we can."

Max paused a moment to regard the bedraggled woman he had just placed in his sister's bed. Her eyes were shuttered closed. Thick dark lashes brushed the tops of her cheekbones in their resting state. Long blonde hair framed her face and covered her shoulders. Even wet, the color reminded him of sunshine and yellow roses. She was beautiful. His traitorous arms ached to hold her, to comfort her, but he would not.

She is married, he reminded himself. Max's gaze held her sleeping form a moment longer before he again noticed the angry red abrasions on her wrists. His body stiffened in anger. *Mother is right. I need time to regroup my thoughts.*

"Thank you, Mother." He stopped just before leaving the room and turned back. "The dog..." He paused and looked at the white bundle of fur curled up next to Maggie. "I must allow Shep to stay here with her. Please make sure the doctor tries to accommodate. She keeps reaching for him. I fear that whatever has transpired, Shep may be Meg's only witness and her biggest comfort."

ACKNOWLEDGMENTS

There are always many people to thank when a book gets written. There are my friends who always cheer me on... Elizabeth Johns, who gave me the push I needed to get started writing, and Betty Phillips, Heather King, Myra Platt, Lauren Smith, and Amanda Mariel, who help in immeasurable ways.

A great big *thank you* goes to my team of readers who spent time and gave up evenings to help me smooth out the rough edges. Thank you, Theresa, Heather, Pat, and Lori! Your help is always greatly appreciated.

And last *but never least*, my *own* hero—my husband and best friend, Roger. He reads every one of my stories.

ABOUT THE AUTHOR

Anna St. Claire is a big believer that *nothing* is impossible if you believe in yourself. She is an emerging author of historical romance and sprinkles her stories with laughter, romance, mystery and lots of possibilities, adhering to the belief that goodness and love will win the day.

Anna is both an avid reader author of American and British historical romance. She and her husband live in Charlotte, North Carolina with their two dogs and often their two beautiful granddaughters, who live nearby. *Daughter, sister, wife, mother, and Mimi*—all life roles that Anna St. Claire relishes and feels blessed to still enjoy. And she loves her pets - dogs and cats alike, and often inserts them into her books as secondary characters.

Anna relocated from New York City to the Carolinas as a small child. Her mother, a retired English and History teacher, always encouraged Anna's interest in writing, after discovering short stories she would write in her spare time.

As a child, she loved mysteries and checked out every Encyclopedia Brown story that came into the school library. Before too long, her fascination with history and reading led her to her first historical romance—Margaret Mitchell's *Gone With The Wind,* now a treasured, but weathered book from being read multiple times. When she discovered Kathleen Woodiwiss,' books, *Shanna* and *Ashes In The Wind,* Anna became hooked. She read every historical romance that came her way and dreams of writing her own historical romances took seed.

Today, her focus is primarily the Regency and Civil War eras, although Anna enjoys almost any period in American and British history. She would love to connect with any of her readers on her website – www.annastclaire.com, through email—annastclaireauthor@gmail.com, Instagram – annast-claire_author, BookBub – www.bookbub.com/profile/anna-st-claire,Twitter – @1AnnaStClaire, Facebook – https://www.facebook.com/authorannastclaire/ or on Amazon – https://www.amazon.com/Anna-St-Claire/e/B078WMRHHF?ref=.

ALSO BY ANNA ST. CLAIRE

The Earl She Left Behind

Embers of Anger

Earl of Weston

Silver Bells And Mistletoe

Earl of Bergen

Made in the USA
Las Vegas, NV
03 December 2024

13225126R00125